The Mustangers

Also by Gary McCarthy

THE LAST BUFFALO HUNT
MUSTANG FEVER
THE DERBY MAN
SHOWDOWN AT SNAKEGRASS JUNCTION
THE FIRST SHERIFF

The Mustangers

GARY McCARTHY

DOUBLEDAY & COMPANY, INC.
GARDEN CITY, NEW YORK
1987

All the characters in this book
are fictitious, and any resemblance
to actual persons, living or dead,
is purely coincidental.

Library of Congress Cataloging in Publication Data

McCarthy, Gary.
The mustangers.

I. Title.
PS3563.C3373M8 1987 813'.54 86-23993

ISBN: 0-385-23855-x

Printed in the United States of America
First Edition

For Ted Fauvre

The Mustangers

CHAPTER ONE

Pete Sills removed his Stetson and sleeved sweat from his brow, then yanked the hat back down tight on his forehead. His dark brown eyes surveyed the high desert and he could feel his heart pounding faster as the dust storm swept in on them and the earth began to tremble.

They are coming, he thought. Any second now they will bust over that ridge and it will be the most beautiful sight in the world. He leaned forward in his stirrups as his horse fidgeted and tossed its head with nervous excitement.

"Listen to 'em," Jack Kendall said, his voice raspy from years of desert and prairie dust and thirst. "Goddamn, I'll bet the boys have chased out thirty of them from them low piñon hills!"

Pete nodded, turning his head to watch the excitement grow in the man who'd taught him everything he knew—maybe ever would know—about mustanging. Even at age forty-two, Jack was still the best broncbuster and mustanger in western Nevada. Pete studied him with pride and thought, I'm riding with a legend.

Jack eased his horse back a little more into the rocks and out of sight. The mustangs would be pushed down into the valley and then driven another few miles up its entire length to be trapped in the immense catch corrals at the far end—they hoped. Getting out of the hills and running was only half the battle, getting them into the corral was the real delicate part. That's why he and Jack were waiting at this junction, waiting to cut the stallion off if he sensed the trap and wanted to lead his band out of the valley.

Even Jack was tense. "I just hope they got the right band," he whispered. "Candy Tyson isn't the kind of girl who likes to be disappointed."

Pete understood him very well. While catching these mustangs today was important, the success of everything they had done this month really depended on whether or not they captured the palomino stallion Candy had already named Sun Dancer and had set her heart on racing in next year's county fair. Sun Dancer was a bolt of lightning, a flash of gold with a flaxen mane and tail and a spirit that challenged any man on horseback to catch him—if he had the talent, the will and most of all, the heart.

Right now, Candy and her father were hiding down near the huge fan-shaped catch corral, waiting and expecting to slam the gates on the palomino stallion and his band of mares. Pete could close his eyes for an instant and almost picture Candy's face etched with fierce determination to own Sun Dancer. He knew he could not allow her to be disappointed.

"There he is!" Pete shouted, forgetting his composure and grinning broadly. The thundering band of mustangs exploded over the rocky ridge and Pete whistled in admiration. "Look at him fly!"

The stallion was driving his band of mares, nipping at the stragglers, then racing forward with head high and urging them not to give up!

"What I wouldn't give for that horse myself," Jack said, almost with reverence. "In thirty years of mustanging, I've never seen a finer stallion. There isn't an animal in Nevada that could touch him in a horse race."

"What if he leaves the mares when he realizes there is a trap ahead?"

Jack shook out his rope and formed a loop. "He won't. He'll stay with his mares and his offspring. I have been watchin' mustang stallions too many years not to have learned something about the way they behave. Some are cowards that will leave their mares, but this is sure not one of them. Get ready, Pete, here they come!"

Pete was ready, had been ready ever since last winter when he and Candy had ridden out and caught a glimpse of the palomino. Candy told him then that it was the horse of her dreams; he wished he could have told her she was the girl of his dreams, but he could not. He wasn't worthy of the love of his boss's daughter—not yet. Not until he had proven he could help catch and ride that golden horse. Trouble was, Jack Kendall was the top broncbuster and it did not seem likely he would let his assistant break the finest wild stallion in Nevada.

"Let's go!" Jack shouted. He was big and strong and he drove his spurs into the ribs of his horse. They shot out from behind the rocks and went scrambling down the mountainside.

The idea was to kill any thoughts of the stallion taking a detour before they came to its mind, but Pete figured his most immediate concern was just staying in the saddle and keeping his horse from losing its footing and turning somersaults all the way down into the valley. The mountainside was murderously steep and covered with shale and every inch of it was moving. Pete knew that if he fell, they would be overtaken in an avalanche of loose rock and buried alive.

"Yah!" Jack bellowed as his horse finally struck level ground and he streaked off toward the stallion.

Pete stayed right on Jack's tail, though it took every bit of skill he possessed to ride down a moving mountainside. Finally reaching flat, solid ground, he reined his horse to press the band of mustangs, and he was sorry that Candy hadn't seen their daredevil horsemanship. He and Jack Kendall were the best horsemen in this part of the country; they could ride stirrup to stirrup with anyone. Pete knew a man didn't get to be Jack's assistant if he were anything less than a spectacular rider with the potential to become a legendary broncbuster.

When the palomino saw them closing distance on a tight angle, its ears flattened and Pete saw its teeth flash as it snaked around to the opposite side of the band. Pete's inclination was to rein his horse and go after the leader but Jack squelched that idea when he yelled, "Let him run free. As long as he is over there, he can't drive the herd anyplace but straight ahead!"

Pete nodded because that made a world of good sense. There were four cowboys behind the band but their horses were about played out. Not only had they beaten the brush and hillsides and hazed the band into a stampede, but they had pushed the mustangs to the limits of their own mounts. Now those cowboys were falling back, smart enough not to go and ruin good saddle horses like some greenhorn with his first taste of mustang fever.

The band was in desperate shape. Up close, Pete could see their distended nostrils and hear their tortured breathing. He knew that the foals and the old mares had long since fallen out and what was left was good, strong stock, horses worth breaking either for the Cross T Ranch, or for the United States Army. Back East, there was a terrible Civil War being fought, and the Union was getting cavalry and wagon horses wherever it could find them. Pete didn't like to think that these mares might someday be ripped apart by cannonfire, but Jack and the boss had told him that it was a possibility, explaining that the Union Army could not be victorious without good horses—not that Mr. Tyson gave a damn about much except piles of money—Yankee, Confederate or otherwise.

"Watch that bay mare!" Jack shouted a warning.

Pete reined away just as the bay collapsed as if someone had shot away her legs. She flipped and Pete heard the sickening *pop* of her neck bones. Pete swore bitterly. Running mustangs like this was a terrible waste of horseflesh; the weak ones gave up and returned to the hills but the strong ones were oftentimes destroyed with busted legs and necks, burst hearts and lungs.

"Ease off a little!"

Pete reined in and pulled his bandanna up close around his eyes. The dust was choking thick and the hooves of the mustangs were throwing tiny rocks and gravel into his face. He tried to tip his hat down for protection but then he could not see. Pete swung his horse out of the boiling dust cloud far enough to breathe clean air. He lifted in his saddle to see the corral up ahead.

The corral itself was impressive. It stood better than ten feet high, just to keep the stallion from having any ideas about trying to leap it and maybe impaling himself to death in the attempt. Pete and the Cross T crew had followed Jack Kendall's direction and constructed it with big timbers hauled clear in from the lumber mills along the Carson River south of Carson City. Pete figured you could stampede a herd of elephants into that corral and its sides would bounce them around plenty before they would splinter.

As impressive as the corral itself was, however, the wings funneling the mustangs into it now counted the most. Each a quarter of a mile long, they fanned out like a pair of open arms from the corral gate. At their extremity, they were nearly three hundred yards across because no mustang in the world would allow itself to be threaded into a narrow funnel.

They had a mile to go. Pete eased his galloping horse up and then reined it directly in behind the band of mares, just the way Jack had taught him to do. Not too close so you'd kill any at this critical moment or risk splitting them off into two bands, but enough to keep them running hard and straight.

Sun Dancer suddenly realized what lay ahead. One moment he was running beside his band and the next he was driving into the mares, punishing them with his teeth and trying to divide them, to make them veer out of the path that would rob them of their freedom.

This was what Pete and Jack had been afraid might happen. The stallion was going to fight. He was going to kill himself if necessary to split his mares and scatter them off the valley floor and into the hills. Pete and Jack went after him at exactly the same instant. Closing in from both sides, they swung their grass ropes and screamed to distract the palomino and take away its authority.

Another mare went down as Pete sliced into the band. His horse momentarily lost its footing and almost fell, but he instinctively jerked its head up and somehow kept the animal erect. He and Jack threw their ropes and both scored as their loops settled over the stallion's powerful neck.

"Stretch 'em out!" Jack yelled.

They dallied and peeled away in opposite directions and the stallion was suddenly pulled between them. It screamed in defiance, unwilling to desert its mares, now unable to drive them to safety. Pete saw a terrible mixture of fear and crazed hatred burn in the stallion's eyes. For a moment, he was almost tempted to throw his rope away and let the animal erupt from the band and attempt to free itself. A horse like that ought to run wild—that was Jack Kendall's opinion, and if it hadn't been for Candy Tyson, Pete guessed it would have been his own as well.

But Pete held the rope and now they were sweeping into the wings of the trap, plunging and sliding and thundering straight toward the maw of the great catch corral.

Pete's rope accidentally caught a desperately weary mare under the neck and jerked its head up. The rope, taut between the stallion and his saddle horn, almost lifted the mare off her front feet as it bit deeply into her throat. She was going to fall, be trampled to death and perhaps bring more down with her.

Pete waited until the very last instant and then he unwound his rope and let it fly, knowing that it was all right, that there was no time for the stallion to break free from his mares and escape. Jack Kendall threw him an angry, questioning look and then, as the mustangs swept into the corral, he cast free his own rope and yanked on his reins, bringing his lathered horse to a sliding stop just outside the corral gate.

Sun Dancer slammed into the opposite wall of the corral and reversed directions faster than a puma before he lunged back into the middle of his band, knocking mares to the earth as he streaked toward the open gate and freedom. The sight of that fire-breathing stallion, all eleven hundred pounds of fury and muscle, with his ears flattened and his teeth bared, was enough to make any man leap for safety.

Pete and Jack could not have unloaded from their horses fast enough to grab the big swinging gate and close it before the stallion smashed into it and trampled them to death. Many a lone mustanger had died, his chest crushed by a gate splintered under the hooves of a half-crazed stallion bent on freedom.

Tyson and Candy had been hiding behind a pile of cut timber and now they were racing to grab and slam the gate shut. It was dangerous work and Pete didn't understand why the boss let his daughter do it, but now, as the gate closed and was barred an instant before Sun Dancer struck it, it was all right. He and Jack drove their horses forward and yanked their Stetsons from their heads and slapped at the palomino until it whirled and began to race around and around the corral.

"We did it!" Candy shouted, hugging her father and bouncing up and down as if she was a little girl. "Sun Dancer is mine!"

"Damn right he is," Tyson said proudly. "You are going to ride the finest piece of horseflesh in this part of the country. Ain't that right, Jack?"

The mustanger nodded, his face thoughtful and a little troubled. "We're going to try and do a job on him, but you know as well as I do that a stallion like that might never be trustworthy. You see those claw scars coming down both shoulders? That horse had a cat on his back, probably when he was just a colt. It's going to make him even harder to ride and train."

"But you can do it, Jack." Candy's smile had evaporated. "You know how long I've wanted this stallion."

"Sure, but you have to understand that a horse like this can never be completely trusted. I just wish you'd look at some of those fillies and young mares, Candy. There are a couple of them that are . . ."

"I've seen them!" She lowered her voice. "Sun Dancer is my horse. Once you geld him, he'll become gentle."

"I wouldn't bet my life on it," Jack snapped.

Hugh Tyson was as big as Jack, only he'd gone soft around the belly and jowls. But he and Jack had once ridden and busted broncs together; they'd been partners and Tyson knew the risks involved in trying to break a stallion like the palomino.

Now he looked at Jack and said in a voice edged with

authority, "I don't pay you to disappoint my daughter, Jack. I know you'll do your best and if that isn't good enough, we'll give the stallion to Pete and let him have a fair try."

Jack flushed deeply. His eyes hardened and he gripped his saddle horn. "You do whatever the hell you want. You pay the wages, but when the day comes that you think Pete here is ready to take my place, I want to be the first man to know."

Tyson nodded. He wrung the anger out of himself and tried to rekindle a friendship grown as cold as the coals of yesterday's campfire. "Nobody stays a broncbuster forever, Jack. You've been damn lucky all these years."

"Luck ain't got a hell of a lot to do with my work. The reason I can still walk is because I don't take foolish chances. I think giving Candy that palomino is a bad mistake, one I don't want to see you live to regret."

Tyson went white around the lips and turned away to yell orders at his other riders. Pete scuffed his toe on the hard dirt and kept his eyes on the stallion. He knew that something mean was building between Jack and Mr. Tyson. Pete wished he could take some measure of feeling good in the fact that the boss had said he trusted him enough to take over one of these days as the Cross T's top broncbuster and mustanger, but he couldn't. Not anymore, he couldn't. A year ago he would have been strutting around like a damned peacock over the chance to step into Jack's boots, but not since he had come to know and respect the man.

"Pete?"

He looked at Candy Tyson.

"If you aren't careful, you're going to get caught crosswise between my father and Jack Kendall. If that happens, I hope you remember that it is my father and this ranch that pay your wages and not Jack."

He gripped the corral rails. "Those are some fine-looking animals in there, Miss Tyson. The other hands will be wanting us to break them a few for our own remuda."

"You'll have to speak to my father about that," she told him, now all smiles. "Look at Sun Dancer! See how proud he is! I can't wait to ride him, Pete. Ever since the first day I laid eyes on that stallion, I've dreamed of winning the horse race at the fair in Reno. You think he will win?"

Pete wanted to comfort her fears and yet not build false hopes. Caught between those two desires, he decided to do what he did best and that was to tell the God's honest truth.

"Miss Tyson, that stallion is the fastest thing I ever saw on four legs, but it takes more than raw speed to win a horse race. It takes want and it takes training."

"Training is your job."

"Yeah, it is, but Jack and I can only do so much. That horse may look like a world-beater out here on the desert floor, leaping over rocks and sage, but on a flat track with other horses all around him, he may not give a . . ."

"A damn? Is that what you were going to say?"

"Yes, ma'am. That and the fact that there are always a few blooded Eastern horses from Kentucky and Tennessee that can fly like the wind."

"I know that," she said with obvious impatience. "But not at next year's fair. In case you've forgotten, the South is at war."

Pete swallowed hurt pride that she should talk to him as if he were ignorant of anything outside this range. He and every cowboy on the spread had struggled with the dilemma of staying out West and not joining up to fight in a war they did not understand over issues they cared little about. Slavery meant nothing to them; black, red and brown men were all over the West and judged on their own merit. Cotton and politics? Pete had no urge to kill soldiers over those kinds of things. He was accustomed to settling differences with his fists. It seemed a better way.

Pete squared his broad shoulders. He was six feet tall and going to be big someday, but right now he was feeling bad over the way Miss Tyson had spoken to him. "I remember about the Civil War back there, but horses don't make war and a few Southerners will bring their best race animals out West thinking that they might escape having them confiscated as officers' mounts. I'm just trying to warn you not to already start counting your money."

She laughed happily. "I don't want to hear any more of your warnings. Leave that kind of talk to Jack Kendall and tell me how great a horse this is going to be. Or would you rather tell that to Maria Kelly?"

He blushed, looked away quickly. Candy's laughter echoed in his ears as she sauntered off. Pete drew a deep breath and leaned his head against the top pole of the corral for a moment. My God, he thought miserably, when did she learn about me seeing Maria late on Saturday nights?

Jack shouted at him to come and help and Pete climbed back on his horse feeling as if his world had ended and knowing that maybe it just had. Jack would be furious at Tyson's remarks about giving a younger man a chance and Pete knew he would take the brunt of that misdirected anger. But a hundred times worse, Candy had discovered he was taking Maria out for moonlight walks. He had started doing that almost a year ago when he had never dreamed that Candy might notice he even existed. But now Candy was showing him interest and if he ever became top broncbuster on the ranch, well . . .

Pete angrily shook the thought away. Jack had been totally unselfish in helping him become as good as he was today. He owed Jack Kendall one hell of a lot. But even so, when it got down to the bare truth of it, a man had to go with the outfit paying his wages.

CHAPTER TWO

Pete knew the first task they faced was to go into the corral and rope the palomino stallion, then drop and tie it or it would keep driving its mares around and around the corral in a constant state of frenzy. If he had any professional weaknesses, Pete felt it might be in his rope work. A broncbuster had to be able to catch and throw outlaw horses before he could get close enough to bridle and saddle them. Roping took a lot of practice and Pete did not like that because it seemed dull. To learn to rope, you needed to be roping something alive and moving, not some bush or corral post. But Jack figured differently and sometimes made him spend at least two hours a day practicing his roping tosses. Pete chafed but he could not argue with the logic that a man entering a corral with a fighting stallion had damn sure better not miss his throw or someone was going to get hurt.

Now, as he rode nervously into the corral with Jack, he was grateful for all those long hours he'd spent with his rope. It was going to be his job to catch the stallion's fore-legs, and Jack was going to rope the hind legs. Then they'd dally and head off in opposite directions. If everything worked according to plan, the stallion ought to drop hard and stay down until some of the other boys got a gunnysack laced down tightly over its eyes and its legs fastened to-gether so it could not possibly break loose. With the stallion taken care of, they could prepare to drive the band of mares across the long miles to ranch headquarters.

"Don't miss," Jack warned in a low voice, "or he'll come at us with everything he has left."

Pete nodded. Everyone, including Candy, was on the rail watching and if Pete missed and the stallion climbed up his back, not only were he and his poor horse going to have a rough time, but Jack might never team up with him again. In this business, you only got one chance and after that, you got hurt bad. Almost as important, Pete simply did not want to look like a fool before the boss and Miss Candy.

"Draw the stud out," Jack said. "Let him know that you are the man that is going to do the job on him. Now he sees you, here he comes!"

The palomino stallion came at him fast, scattering his mares like a cannonball scorching through a covey of quail. One minute Sun Dancer was over against the far rails snorting and pawing, the next his ears were down flat on his golden head and his long yellow teeth were coming to take Pete's head off.

The throw was tricky and it had to be perfectly coordinated between him and Jack or it would fail. Jack was damn near foolproof and it was assumed by everyone watching that if there were any mistakes made, they would be Pete's.

When the stallion broke through his band of mares, Pete's arm shot forward low and out from his body and the loop formed a figure-eight loop; it snaked down and sailed along the hard-packed earth so that it seemed as if the palomino stepped right through both loops with his sharp forehooves. Everyone watching knew that the toss was the product of a thousand hours of practice and that only a broncbuster trained personally by Jack Kendall could be expected to make it when the chips were down.

Pete timed his pull upward on the rope exactly to the

right moment and the loops caught both legs just over the fetlocks. At the same instant, Jack came streaking in from the side and his own loop caught the hind legs and all of a sudden the stallion found itself lifting off the ground in the back end and then Pete's rope was jerking it sideways and forward.

The horse went down hard. Pete heard the breath whoosh out of those great lungs and before the stallion could recover its senses, a knot of cowboys were flying through the rails and landing on the palomino's neck, pinning its thrashing head to the dirt and blinding it with the gunnysack. A moment later, thick leather hobbles were cinched up around the mustang's hocks and it was rendered nearly harmless—if you stayed back from those blindly snapping teeth.

Both Jack and Pete urged their horses forward a little and released enough slack so that the cowboys could free their ropes.

"Goddamn!" Tyson yelled. "You won't see any better team-roping than that anywhere in the world. Not even the Mex vaqueros could top it!"

Jack said nothing. Pete knew that the legendary broncbuster did not agree. To Jack, nobody handled a rope like the Mexican vaqueros did their riatas. They could make those fifty-foot lengths of braided leather almost catch the legs off flying butterflies.

"Nice work, Pete!"

He looked over to see Candy hanging on to the top rail. "Thanks," he mumbled, coiling up his rope and knowing that the other cowboys had heard that and would be ribbing the devil out of him for days.

Candy jumped into the corral, but Jack spurred his horse forward to block her path. "You shouldn't be in here," he snapped. "A mare could come flying around and tromp you to death!"

"That's my horse," Candy said stubbornly. "I want to take a look at him up close." Then, without waiting for her father to back her up, she moved around Jack's horse and walked over beside the blinded Sun Dancer.

Candy was no starry-eyed city girl. She rode like a Comanche and she knew horses as well as some of the cowboys, but even so, Pete could not help but feel his gut tighten up as she put her hand on that big palomino. At the touch of her fingers, the animal squealed as if he had been prodded with a red-hot branding iron. The stallion's head came up and those teeth of his snapped like the jaws of a steel bear trap. He just missed Candy's arm and she retreated to the fence, her face very pale.

No one said a word except Jack. "Goddamn crazy to let her have that horse! He might just kill her before this is all finished."

Candy glared at him in hurt and anger.

"Let's get the mares ready," Tyson said, breaking the tension. "As it is, we'll be lucky to reach the Cross T by sundown. Come on, boys!"

Everyone seemed glad to move, especially Pete. As Jack Kendall's assistant and the one who would have a fair piece of the responsibility for saddle-breaking these mares, he had some authority and he was not afraid to use it. "Jones, get the sacking for their eyes. Ed, you get the chains and the rest of you men pair up and start working them."

The cowboys didn't argue. Maybe some of the older ones didn't like the idea of taking orders from a nineteen-year-old, but Pete had earned enough respect by breaking horses to make them listen.

With the stallion tied and blindfolded, the mares were suddenly without a leader and the rebellion went right out of them. They were roped by two riders, then sacked, and a leather band with a twelve-inch chain was buckled just over a rear hock. As soon as the mare tried to run, the chain would begin to slap its delicate leg bones, and after a very few minutes, the mustang understood that it could walk but not run without immediate self-inflicted pain. Blinded, chained and tied together head to tail, they were soon ready for the return trip to Cross T.

"Head them out!" Tyson yelled to his men. "Let's go, Candy."

"I'd like to help Pete and Jack."

"No," her father said abruptly. "We're shorthanded and the boys need us."

Candy was disappointed and so was Pete, who had been hoping all morning that he might spend one moonlit night riding beside her, even if Jack Kendall was alongside as a chaperon.

Candy frowned. "You don't geld him before you get to the ranch."

"Be easier to handle if we got it over with," Jack said, his tone blunt and stubborn.

"No! He might bleed to death."

"Been a long time since that happened to one of mine," Jack said, obviously trying to keep his temper from getting out of hand.

"Just the same," Tyson interrupted, "I think I'll call out the vet from Yerington."

Jack stiffened. He had gelded dozens of stallions but was too proud to argue the point. All he said was, "You got money to waste, Hugh, then waste it."

Tyson's meaty face flushed with anger. "You're going to push me too far, Jack."

"No, I'm not because after this horse is broke, I'm drawing my pay and riding out. You can give my job to Pete."

"You'd quit me? After all we been through?" Now that it

had been said, it seemed obvious that Tyson was hurt and surprised.

"Because of all we've been through," Jack corrected. "No sense in stompin' an old friendship to pieces any longer. I'm leaving before we end up killing each other."

Tyson reached for his whiskey and took a long drink. He looked bitter. His eyes were bloodshot and his face was twisted with fury. When he spoke, his voice shook. "Yeah," he said, "I think you'd damn well better do that."

So, finally, it was done. Pete took a deep breath and let it out slowly. Jack was leaving and Pete knew it was the best thing to do. If he didn't, those two would have fought—and by the look in Tyson's eyes, it would have been with guns. But to Pete, the thought of Jack not being a big part of the Cross T Ranch was hard to swallow. And as for the promotion, he didn't want it nearly enough to see his friend ride away.

"Pete, I'm counting on you to make sure that horse arrives safely," Candy said.

Pete nodded but he didn't take his eyes off Jack, so Candy just rode away.

Jack rolled a smoke and stood beside the corral, hardly bothering to watch as the last of the mustangs were lined out toward ranch headquarters. When he finished his cigarette, he ground it out, then he rolled a second one and smoked it slower. Pete had never seen him smoke two in a row like that. He guessed that Jack was pretty angry inside.

"Maybe you didn't mean what you said about leaving, huh, Jack."

"You know I did."

Pete frowned. "But this is home! Everybody sort of flies off the handle sometimes and says things that they regret later. I could tell that Mr. Tyson didn't want you to quit. He'd forget you even offered."

"He can do what he damn sure pleases," Jack replied, heading back into the corral. "But I'm quitting as soon as this palomino stud is safe for Candy to ride."

Jack had a rope in his hand and he knelt beside the stallion, talking low in a singsong way that was just as gentle as a mother soothing her baby. He always talked like that to broncs; Pete had listened hard to catch the words but they made no sense to him. Maybe they were Indian or just something made up that Jack figured sounded reassuring to a frightened wild horse. No matter what language, they worked. Pete had never seen a horse that Jack couldn't calm with his voice and Sun Dancer was no exception. The golden stallion was breathing hard and you could see his pulse was racing but that was due to fear rather than exertion.

Pete felt the claw marks across the palomino's withers and down his muscular shoulders. "It's a wonder this horse survived."

Jack didn't answer. He slipped his noose over the front hoof and pulled it tight just under the fetlock. Next, he brought the rope up and with considerable effort they managed to tie that foreleg against the stallion's chest.

By the time they were finished, Sun Dancer was getting pretty excited again and Jack was moving quickly. "All right," he said, picking up the end of one of his ropes that was still around the stallion's neck and motioning Pete to take the other. "Let's get mounted and let him come up on three legs."

And that is what they did. Sun Dancer surged to his feet, and even though he was still blindfolded by the gunnysack and one of his forelegs was tied, he was a wildcat. He tried to shake loose of the ropes around his neck. Failing that, the palomino threw himself into the air and came down hard. Pete was watching Jack's face and when the stallion landed and that single front leg did not break or even buckle, the broncbuster smiled.

"Keep your rope tight and let's ease on out the gate. Try to keep him from going over backward. We got to bring this one in without a scratch."

Pete did not need to be reminded. So they led the fighting stallion out and through those long wings toward the ranch. After a tough mile, Sun Dancer began to settle down. It wasn't because he was giving up, but rather because he seemed to understand that fighting wasn't going to be of any use, not blinded and on three legs.

They had several bad moments during those first few miles when they passed the dead mares that had collapsed during the chase or stepped into a badger hole and cartwheeled under the hooves of the running band. Tyson and his cowboys had mercifully put them out of their misery, but the stallion could smell his mares and obviously identify each one. Pete watched its ears move back and forth and saw its nostrils quiver at the death scent; he and Jack had to pull the stallion on past and it made both of them feel terrible.

Mustanging was a tough, dirty business and a dangerous one as well. It took its toll on men and horses and yet there were few ways better or faster to catch horses than simply running them down and roping them or stampeding them into a waiting trap.

Time passed and the warm summer sun dove into the Sierra Nevada Mountains and the stars began to pop up out of the night sky and twinkle brightly. A half-crescent moon floated across the heavens like some ancient Nordic sailing vessel and the ageless Nevada hills echoed noisily with the song of the coyote. The stallion had settled down enough so that they had untied its raised foreleg but kept it blinded and their ropes stretched tight. They were making good time now, and maybe they would beat midnight by a couple of hours.

"You know what I think, Pete?"

He studied Jack's silhouette. Framed against the heavens, riding his horse as if the two were a single moving piece of flesh and bone, Pete felt a sudden ache in his throat when he realized the man was actually riding on. Pete did not even trust his voice to answer.

"I think I'm mighty glad to be leaving," Jack said. "Sometimes a man stays too long in one place, he gets lazy in mind and body."

"Lazy is something you'll never be."

"I've always tried to earn my wages. It's just that we all get into comfortable habits, Pete. And that ain't the best thing for us. You follow what I'm trying to say?"

"Yeah. You're telling me that I should come along with you and maybe I just will!"

"No!"

His voice stung Pete to anger. "Well, why the hell not! We make a fair enough team of mustangers, don't we?"

Jack nodded and his voice softened. "Sure we do, son, but this is your chance to run the show. It'll do you good to get the experience. I'm tired of tellin' you what to do when you already know. I need some dumb bastards to order around."

Pete had to smile and sit up a little straighter in the saddle. Not being a "dumb bastard" meant he set pretty well in Jack's eyes.

"Tell you one thing," Jack said, rolling a cigarette with one hand. "I'm going to miss this rough old high desert country, though. I got a war bag full of memories scattered hereabouts."

Pete had heard them all, but he wanted to hear them all over again. "Such as?"

"I remember the first time Hugh and I saw a band of mustangs being brought into Reno to be shipped by rail to the slaughterhouses in Chicago. We were sitting on the porch with our boots up on the rail, drinking beer. But when we seen those horses, we both dropped our beers and just stared."

Pete waited as long as he could stand it and then grew impatient. "What was wrong with them?"

"What was wrong? I'll tell you. Them cowboys had beaten hell out of the mustangs and then blindfolded them, but the part neither Hugh or I could tolerate was that they had wired their nostrils shut so that they couldn't even breathe!"

Pete flushed. "I never heard of that sort of thing."

"Used to be fairly common. If they can't breathe 'cept through their mouths, they can't run. Another thing they used to do was to cut a tendon or even a knee joint so that the water would drip out and the mustang's knee would freeze up. Of course, these were the poor mustangs, the ones with crooked legs or some other deformity that made them useless under saddle or in harness."

"Still wasn't right," Pete said in a low, hard voice.

"That's what Hugh and I thought. We came out of our chairs at the same time and went out into the street and yanked the nearest two men right out of their saddles and beat the hell out of them in front of God and the whole town."

"Good for you," Pete said fiercely.

"Well, sorta. The rest unloaded and beat us up, but neither Hugh or I ever regretted that day. We got drunk and rowdy and then we rode out of town and never came back. I guess you could say that it was the beginning of our friendship. After that, we stuck together through a lot of hard years."

Pete had never heard Jack open up like this and he was eager to hear more. Maybe if he understood Jack and Hugh Tyson, he could see a way to patch up a friendship.

"Hugh was a pretty good man, huh?" Pete wanted Jack to think about that and remember it some.

"A damn good man. We rode the rough stock together for a lot of good years. Then he met and fell in love with Candy's mother and he changed."

"You mean she ruined him or something?"

"Hell no! He ruined himself. That was the finest lady that ever walked the earth. She was an angel and I'd have married her first if I'd had the chance. But what she did was make Hugh decide that he couldn't stay the same as he had been and that he needed to build something to hang his hat on."

"Like the Cross T."

"Exactly."

"Nothing wrong with that," Pete dared to add.

"No, not as long as you remember what you were and what is right and wrong. For a while Hugh did, but then he started making pretty good money off these mustangs and he changed."

"Can you be sure of that?"

"Hell yes! The man got greedy, he don't give a damn about anything 'cept money anymore. You've seen him. Pete, I don't mean to rile you or anything, but his daughter turned out more like him than her mother."

"I think you're dead wrong."

"Wouldn't be the first time or the last," Jack growled. "But I can't leave you without a warning. I know how you feel about Candy. Hell, she'd turn any man's head. She's flirtatious and damn good-looking. She got her mother's looks, but that's as far as it goes."

"She's good inside, too!" Pete snapped.

"I never said she was bad. I just said she's the wrong girl for you," Jack said stubbornly. "Candy won't ever be yours. Her father wants her to marry a professional man—doctor, lawyer, banker. If he ever figures out that you are thinking about Candy the way you are, he'll fire you quick as a sneeze."

They rode on in silence a few minutes until Pete had to ask, "You ever hear Mr. Tyson say that, or are you just guessing?"

"About Candy marrying an educated and professional man?"

"We're professionals, damn it! I mean about the educated part?"

"He's said it in every way but words. You seen how he's always inviting the young up-and-coming business fellas out here for dinner. He wants Candy to marry into more money. That ought to be plain to see as the ears on a mule."

"I don't believe it."

"Then I feel sorry for you because it's true. The girl for you is Maria Kelly."

"We're just friends." He had heard enough about Maria for one day.

"Not according to her, you aren't."

Pete stiffened in the saddle. "You mean that she told you and Candy both! Damn it, I got to talk to that girl."

"You better think it out real careful first. If you break her heart, I'll come back and break your fool neck. That Maria is special."

Pete fumed in silence.

"You know," Jack said, "one of the great mysteries in this life is that people always want what they shouldn't have and whatever is good for them they either don't want or they take for granted."

Pete clenched his teeth in anger.

"Take this stud, for instance," Jack continued. "If he was mine, it might work out, or if he was yours, you might just make him into something special. But the average hand would either get hurt on him, ruin him, or wind up putting a bullet into his brain. Same goes for Candy. This isn't the horse for her but I did see a young mare in that band that would make her a dandy."

"She isn't interested in taking second-best," Pete said, a little pridefully.

"I understand that," Jack said, "and even though you haven't said it right out, you think Maria is second-best to Candy Tyson. Well, you're wrong. Candy will break your heart or else put it in one of her damned jewelry boxes while Maria would give you the best years of her life. I hope something happens to make you see the truth of what I say."

Pete frowned and did not bother to reply. If Tyson was set on his only child marrying a doctor or such kind of fella, this entire discussion was pointless anyway.

CHAPTER THREE

They moved down Goose-Neck Valley and out of the sage into marsh grass where an underground river flowed out of the Sierras then bled into the high desert. It was a beautiful night and somewhere in the distance another wild stallion trumpeted a shrill challenge to Sun Dancer.

Instantly, the palomino's head lifted, its nostrils distended. It called back, a wild sound filled with its spirit. Pete and Jack had to stop and tie Sun Dancer's foot up again because he got to fighting the ropes so bad they were afraid of choking him to death. It was a starkly beautiful scene, though, that magnificent golden horse pathetically challenging some unseen rival. It made Pete think of what some man might feel being sentenced to a life in prison and then being shackled and led toward the walls of stone and iron that would forever lock him away from the outside world. He listened to the stallion, and even though he knew Sun Dancer would have an easier life, it gave him a sad feeling in the pit of his stomach.

Jack must have felt the same way too, for when they finally got the horse settled down he said, "One like this ought never to be tamed and ridden. He ought to be kept wild and allowed to sire others just like himself."

"Maybe so," Pete said guardedly.

"No maybe about it. If Hugh can't see that clearing the range of its best stallion won't hurt him and the future generations of mustangs in these parts, then he is damned shortsighted. I never wanted to catch this one. I argued like hell to leave him free. You can see why when you look at the mustangs he has fathered. They're a cut above all the rest on this range."

"You think he could win at the fair next year?" Pete asked, wanting to change the subject since the issue was already settled and there was no sense feeling any worse about it than they already did.

Jack chuckled suddenly. "I do. If the palomino decides that's what he wants."

Pete nodded. "You've shown me how to bust a bronc the easy way so as not to kill its spirit. You've shown me how to put a soft mouth and an easy rein on them, too. But how in blazes do we teach Sun Dancer to behave on a racetrack?"

"We don't. We just get him in line and let him run and hope he is fast enough to leave the pack behind. Me, I'd be afraid one like this would eat up a purebred."

"You mean take a hunk out of him?"

"Sure," Jack said. "All this horse has ever done is fight and win. He had to whip some older stud to steal his first mares and you can bet there has not been a week in his life that he didn't tangle with a younger stud wanting to expand his harem. You can see all those scars on him besides the claw marks. This horse is a warrior. That's what he does best and breaking him won't change his instinct to strike without hesitation or warning."

"Could you ever trust him, even after he's been gelded?" Pete was worried about Candy. She was a fine rider, but she was not a professional.

"I don't know. On the other hand, can you ever completely trust another human being when things go to hell? I don't think so."

"I trust you, Jack." He hadn't meant to say that; the words had just popped out of his mouth, and though he was a little embarrassed, they were true and he did not wish them back.

Jack seemed to forget what he was about to say next. He rolled a cigarette as they plodded up the Goose-Neck and, overhead, a flock of ducks sailed across the moon like an empty arrowhead, squawking at the silvery landscape below. It was a long time before either of them spoke again and by then they were almost at the ranch.

Jack cleared his throat. "Just one thing," he said. "Don't ever tell anyone what I told you about Mrs. Tyson."

"About you wishing you could have married her instead of Mr. Tyson?"

"Yeah."

"I won't." Pete figured everyone who knew Jack before Mrs. Tyson had died of cholera had already guessed the broncbuster was in love with his best friend's wife. It was said that after her funeral, Mr. Tyson got drunk and never really sobered up again. It was also said that Jack Kendall got drunk too, but when he sobered up, he got even tougher.

It was after midnight when they came in sight of headquarters. The ranch house and outbuildings formed a horseshoe, and over them towered a hundred beautiful big cottonwood trees. Those cottonwoods were a landmark in this part of the country and everyone knew that Mrs. Tyson had asked her husband to dig them up when they were very small and transplant them from the Carson River. What only three men on Cross T knew—and Pete was one of them—was that Tyson had at first refused. At that time, he hadn't the money or the men to waste on a job that he thought so frivolous. So Jack Kendall, hearing the woman he secretly loved cry and feeling each sob rip at his heart, hitched up a wagon in the night and went to the river alone. And he had returned every night for a week until Tyson couldn't stand it any longer and had joined him in the work.

Mrs. Tyson always thought her husband had relented all on his own and Jack would have rather had his tongue pulled out than let her know the real story.

Jack had never related this story to anyone, but it was the truth and the men of the Cross T knew it and respected the old broncbuster all the more for it. Pete had a theory that Jack had shamed his boss with those trees and Hugh Tyson had never completely forgiven his old friend, who had allowed him the praise and the credit. But the thing that bothered Pete most was that, after all these years, Mr. Tyson had taken to bragging about how it had been his idea to plant those big cottonwood trees.

"We'll put him in the high corral," Jack said as they rode into the yard. "Make sure he has plenty of water and I'll pitchfork in some grass hay. Hope he eats and drinks."

Pete nodded. He knew that captured mustang stallions sometimes chose death rather than lose their freedom.

The door to the ranch house banged open and Candy came running out. "So, you made it after all," she said, pulling open the corral gate as the mares began to whinny with excitement at the sight of their leader.

There were four big circular corrals for mares and saddle-broken horses, and two more that were especially stout, tall and strong, with snubbing posts in the center for busting broncs. Sun Dancer was going into the best of the six corrals, one impossible to escape.

"Is he all right?" Candy asked.

"He sure is," Pete said when Jack didn't bother to answer. "Not a scratch on him. We had a rough time holding him, though, when another stallion bugled a challenge."

She watched from outside as Pete and Jack loosened the blindfold enough so that it would soon fall off of its own accord, then removed their ropes and rode outside. Feeling the ropes free of his neck, Sun Dancer trotted blindly around and around the corral, his shoulder barely touching the rails as he called over and over to his mares.

"He's just going to have to get over them," Candy offered sympathetically. "But I'll try to make it up to him."

Pete killed a grin. He did not think any human could replace the affections of all those pretty mares. Then he thought about Sun Dancer being gelded and he felt a real emptiness in the pit of his stomach. It wasn't a thing that you could talk to a girl about, especially one like Candy Tyson, but it was there all the same.

When he had finished hauling buckets of fresh water to the water trough, then turning his own unsaddled horse out with the others, Pete was ready to hit his bunk. He had been in the saddle for nearly twenty-four hours straight and he wondered how a man Jack's age still managed to sit ramrod-straight and never complain.

Candy, however, fell in beside him as he lugged his saddle toward the tack barn. "You were really something when you roped Sun Dancer by the forelegs."

He lifted his saddle and placed it on a saddle rack where it belonged, then carefully set his horse blankets over it with the sweaty side up so that they would dry quicker.

"Well, thanks," he said. "Jack's toss was a lot more difficult."

"That's not what my father said. Yours was the one that did a figure eight, and you were the one that horse was going to have for supper if you missed. The pressure was all on you, Pete, and you handled it beautifully. Dad and I were very proud of you."

When she said that, she smiled in a way that made his knees feel buttery. Pete grinned and fiddled in the darkness for a moment, adjusting his blankets.

Candy laughed soft and way down deep in her throat before she moved back across the yard. Pete watched her hips swinging and he could hear the cottonwood leaves fluttering in the night breeze at about the same speed as his pulse. He was not sure if he should go after her and walk her back to the house at this late hour, or just knock the dust off his chaps and head for his bunk. He wasn't sleepy anymore.

"You want a drink of water or something?" she asked, turning around, hands resting on her shapely hips.

He kicked himself forward, feeling wooden-legged the way he did after being in the saddle for six or eight straight hours. "You bet!" he said much too eagerly as he began to follow her to the ranch house.

When they reached the front porch, Candy said, "You better wait right here. You know my father's rules about hired hands coming into the house."

"Sure." The only man on the payroll allowed to go inside was Jack Kendall, who avoided the place as if it were haunted by the ghost of the woman he had loved.

"I'll go inside and pour you a little something from Father's private stock."

"Now, wait a minute," he said quickly, "maybe that isn't such a good idea."

"And maybe it's not such a bad one either," she said with a sly wink. "I think this calls for a little celebration and I'm going to have a drink myself."

"You are?" He was stunned.

"That's right. I always have a little drink when there's something special going on around this place, and sometimes . . . sometimes I have a private drink of Father's best whiskey when there isn't a damned thing going on at all!"

She'd shocked him just as she'd expected she would and then laughed as Pete smiled nervously. If Mr. Tyson found him out here on the porch sipping liquor with his daughter in the moonlight, he would get horsewhipped, then fired—and he'd deserve both.

But before he could think of a way to get back to the bunkhouse, she headed inside to get the whiskey. Pete stood up and peered into the house. He cussed himself silently and jammed his fists into his pockets.

Jack sauntered past on his way to the bunkhouse and he stopped about ten yards out and said in a low voice, "You're headed for big trouble, Pete. Best come along with me while you can still turn back. Give her half the chance, she'll want to castrate you just as sure as she does Sun Dancer."

"I can't just walk away now!" he hissed. "I got to stay and at least say goodnight."

"No, you don't. Saying goodnight to the boss's daughter isn't part of your job."

He heard her footsteps in the hallway. "I'll be along in a minute."

"I don't think so," Jack sighed. "Don't say you weren't warned."

Jack continued on and Pete nearly leaped off the porch to go along, but the door swung open and there was Candy, with a tray, two glasses and a crystal decanter of the boss's finest whiskey.

"I'm not much of a drinking man," he said lamely, hoping that she might be looking for a way to take back her invitation.

"That's all right," she told him, placing everything down on a small table. She poured them both two fingers full and handed him a glass, then offered a toast. "To your becoming our top broncbuster."

He drank without enthusiasm.

"You don't look very happy," she said, clearing her throat of the fiery liquor. "What's wrong?"

"I'll miss Jack. Seems to me like he belongs here with us."

"I'll miss him, too," Candy said, "but Jack belongs wherever he wants to be. He made his choice and I hope you've made yours."

"I'm staying."

"Good! Now, let's have another toast to the successful capture of Sun Dancer and to new beginnings."

He drank, wondering what "new beginnings" meant. With Sun Dancer or him?

She emptied her glass. He felt obligated to match her drink for drink, like a gentleman. She refilled them at once and said, "Pete, I think you underestimate your abilities. You are ready to take over the mustanging part of Cross T and you have been for a year or more. You're sweet and a man of great loyalty. Loyalty is very important to my father and me."

He sipped his whiskey, wishing he could get out of this somehow without hurting her feelings or sounding like a fool.

"Do you think I'm pretty?" The question did not come out as casually as she might have hoped.

He almost choked. "Well, yeah, sure! You're beautiful, Candy. Prettiest girl I ever seen."

That pleased her but she said modestly, "I'm not as pretty as my mother was. She was really beautiful, but kind of soft. She let people get away with a lot of things, especially my father."

"Oh." He did not know what he was supposed to say to that.

"Why do you think Jack dislikes me so much?"

The way she asked told Pete more than the question itself. He wanted to say that she was wrong, but that would be lying.

"I don't know." Pete set his glass down. The whiskey was already taking effect. "Miss Tyson, I best say goodnight."

She looked very disappointed and kind of sad, too. "I guess you better go at that. We'll have a big day tomorrow with Sun Dancer. Pete?"

He was afraid of what she was going to ask next.

"How do you really feel about Maria?"

Now he took the decanter and poured himself another glass and swallowed it neat, feeling the fire of it boil up in his guts. When he could make his tongue operate again, he formed an answer. "I think Maria is a fine girl. I like her a lot, but I don't love her."

"But you could."

It was a question he'd asked himself a time or two but never was able to answer. "I don't know." He cleared his throat. "Why do you ask?"

"Just wondering. You must have seen the men that my father has coming out to see me."

"Gentlemen, all of them."

Anger flashed across her pretty face, but she masked it well with forced laughter. "Oh, they do have clean hands, money and nice manners, but most of them don't know anything about horses and aren't interested in learning."

"Maybe what they know is pretty interesting, too," he offered, trying hard to be as fair as he could. "It's a big world, lots of people doing lots of interesting things."

She looked at him strangely. "How would you know? You've spent almost your entire life on the Cross T working with mustangs."

Pete felt a little hurt and offended. The way she said it made it sound as if he didn't know what was going on outside of western Nevada and that just was not true. He read most every old newspaper and book he could lay his hands on.

"Candy, just because I've been here a long time, it doesn't mean I think this is all there is in the world. I've met a lot of cowboys and drifters. All of them tell you about the big cattle towns, the wild mining strikes and places like that. But you know what?"

"What?" she asked with a soft smile.

"The truth of it is that I haven't met one fella that wasn't searching for a place to set his hat and call home."

"And this is your home, Pete! It always will be."

Before he could think of a reply to show his gratitude, her lips were moving against his and her soft, full body was pressing tightly to his own.

Pete had kissed a few girls but none like this! She and the whiskey combined to make him feel as though he wanted to explode.

She eased out of his arms and studied his face with a tender expression. "You know what?"

"What?" he asked thickly.

"After that kiss, I'll expect you to stop seeing Maria Kelly alone."

Pete blinked with shock and surprise. Her words hit him like a washbasin full of ice water. When he recovered his wits enough to speak, he said, "Maria is a friend."

"You've got enough friends in the bunkhouse."

"But . . ."

She kissed him, quick and hard. "Goodnight."

He was too surprised even to open the door before she disappeared inside.

Pete stood rooted in place. He had always placed Candy a notch above himself. She was so damned attractive that men flocked to her. She was better educated and traveled. And she was the boss's daughter. Now he could not imagine what she saw in him, but whatever it was, he hoped it would last. Pete licked his lips, tasting a little of her again. He felt almost dizzy with exhilaration and the stars seemed so dazzling that he actually reached up and tried to pluck one from the heavens for Candy.

"Peter?"

He spun around to see Maria standing in the shadows beside the rose garden she and her mother tended. She had a soft, lilting voice that was now filled with unspeakable sorrow. Pete groaned to realize she had been watching, maybe even heard the conversation he had just shared with Candy.

"Peter, please, I want to talk with you."

He slowly walked to her as his mixed feelings roiled like a troubled river deep inside. He did not want to hurt this girl's feelings. Always, because she had worked for Cross T the same as he did and neither of them had known their natural fathers, there had been a strong bond between them. They had explored the land, fished, swum and shared favorite dogs and horses. Maria had once saved his life when the horse he was racing beside her suddenly stepped in a prairie dog hole and somersaulted. Maria had stopped the bleeding and then had gone for help. They were like brother and sister, and yet . . . yet there had always been something more that neither of them could deny. A trust, perhaps even an unspoken promise that they might someday start a new life as husband and wife.

Candy had suddenly changed all that and Pete felt a little guilty, as if he was a betrayer. "Maria, why did you have to be out here tonight?"

She raised her chin. "Because I knew what she was going to do."

He was impatient to leave. "That doesn't even make sense."

"To me it does. I have seen her with many men before. A

woman can tell those things. You are not the first she has kissed that way and you will not be the last."

"I don't want to listen to this. Go inside and go to bed."

"I heard her say that you are not to see me alone again," Maria whispered, her voice close to breaking. "How can she do that!"

He took a deep, ragged breath. "No one can tell me who to see or not see," he told her. "We'll still be friends."

"But I love you!"

"Yes, I know that," he admitted quietly, "but you have to understand that I love . . ."

Before he could say it, Maria covered his mouth with her eager lips. Pete struggled only for a moment and then he relaxed, feeling the softness of her and knowing it was terrible of him to be kissing two different girls in the space of five minutes.

Maria's kiss seemed as though it would never end and he wasn't about to stop it. But when things seemed about to get carried away, Pete gently disengaged her arms from around his neck.

Her black eyes glistened wetly and she was breathing hard. "I am the one for you!" she said fiercely. "And you better learn that pretty damn quick!"

She whirled and raced back inside to leave Pete alone and smelling her perfume, tasting her mouth instead of Candy's.

Pete was dazed. He barely managed to get headed in the right direction toward the bunkhouse. Too much had happened too fast. He needed to sleep and then think. And out in the corral, Sun Dancer whinnied to his mares. The stallion was probably just as confused and upset as Pete—and they both had very good reasons.

CHAPTER FOUR

Pete reviewed the conversation he'd shared with Candy Tyson until almost dawn when he gave up and drifted to sleep for a few hours. Now, as he staggered into the cookshack and sat down at the rough wooden table and bench, all he wanted was coffee and a chance to wake up.

Old Peewee Blake had already run the other cowboys out and was boiling dishwater on the stove. Peewee was tough and ill-tempered and ran his cookshack like an Army sergeant. The only two men he was inclined to socialize with were Pete and Jack Kendall because he had once been a broncbuster himself. A lot of bad spills had left him crippled in the knees and the small of his back, so Pete knew he was in constant and considerable pain. Peewee was only forty-seven years old but he looked sixty because he had traveled from one ranch to another as a contract buster, riding outlaws—horses no one else could stick.

Contract busters were paid by the head and they were often called "bronc fighters," a term that a man like Jack held in contempt. All a bronc fighter cared about was staying in the saddle long enough to break a mustang's spirit before it broke his bones. Horses rode out by bronc fighters were never much good; they were often resentful, cowering critters, sneaky and prone to buck on cold mornings.

The broncbuster took more time with his horses since he wasn't paid by the number he rode. He gentled them, taught them not to buck and made sure they turned out to be pretty good handling horses. Pete could usually tell whether a horse had been broken by a bronc fighter or buster, and so could most cowboys who had to live with the result. He and Jack Kendall were the main reasons why Cross T horses always brought top dollar in the saleyard or out at Fort Churchill as cavalry replacement mounts.

Peewee shoved a cup of coffee across the table. "It's down to the grounds, Pete, but I saved you and Jack a cup or two each."

Pete knuckled his bloodshot eyes and wished he hadn't drunk whiskey last night with Candy. Even the good stuff tasted bad the morning after. "Jack been in yet?"

"Nope. I think he is out there getting fixed up to ride that palomino stallion this morning."

Pete sipped at the scalding coffee. He had better hurry on out there to help Jack rope Sun Dancer.

"Here comes trouble," Peewee grunted.

Pete didn't turn around when he heard the boots thumping on the rough pine floor. "Trouble" was the new cattle boss by the name of Lester Barron that Tyson hired a week ago. Lester was a big, loudmouthed New Mexico cowboy who'd alienated everyone on the Cross T the moment he'd delivered five thousand head of longhorn cattle to the ranch and then had gotten himself and his men hired to oversee them. Tyson already had a small crew of cowboys to work his cattle, but when they learned they'd be taking orders from Lester, they'd quit.

Fortunately, the cattle were separate from the mustanging and neither Pete, Jack nor any of their horsemen had been forced to endure Lester's bossy ways. If they had, they'd have drawn their wages and quit, too.

Lester had a surprisingly high-pitched voice for a really big man, and it carried like a bell. "Pete," he squawked, "you better talk to that hardheaded old son of a bitch or there's going to be trouble this morning."

Pete stiffened. He turned to face Lester and the humorless kind of men who always seemed to clutter his wake. "Who are you talking about?"

"Jack Kendall, who else! He's set his mind on breaking that palomino this morning."

"Then I better help him."

Lester blocked the doorway. He was taller than Pete by three inches and his face was battle-scarred. Lester talked tough and Pete was pretty sure he could back up his words.

"The boss wants you mustangin' boys to hold off breaking that palomino stud."

"How do you know that?"

" 'Cause he said so when I went up to the house early this morning. Seems we're going to have us a rodeo next Sunday."

"A what!"

"A rodeo. And that stud is going to bury Jack for the crowd before me and my hands put on a roping show like they've never seen before."

Pete finished his coffee in a single gulp. He had no intention of arguing with Lester this morning, not when Jack needed help. There had already been one fight between a New Mexico cowboy and one of the mustangers over who was the better crew of ropers. What it came down to, Pete thought, was that the cowboys were better with cattle and the mustangers were better roping horses. That seemed reasonable. But what he also believed was that it took a whole lot more skill and practice to rope a pair of flying forelegs than it did to rope those big cow horns.

"Are you going to stop him or am I?" Lester demanded.

"Neither of us will if he don't want to be stopped. But I'll try."

"The hell with that! Kendall has already quit, hasn't he? As far as I see it, he's just extra baggage that needs cleaning out."

A cowboy tapped Lester on the shoulder.

"What do you want?" he hissed at the man.

"Just to say that, on account of how everyone here thinks that palomino is so special and old Jack is the best, we better not run him off. Like it or not, riding that bronc is going to be a show that will attract the crowds."

Lester frowned. "Makes sense," he finally conceded, stepping aside to allow Pete to go by. "But you'd better talk him out of riding this morning or else I damn sure will!"

Pete strode on past the man feeling hackles rise on his neck. As he approached the corrals, one of his mustangers came up running. The man's name was Earl and Pete trusted him to know what was really going on. "Is it true the boss wants us to hold off breaking Sun Dancer?"

"That's right. Mr. Tyson allowed as how we can send out the word and do it next Sunday. We'll get a hell of a crowd out here and have a little fun. The betting will be fierce."

"Jack can ride anything with hair."

"He may have met his equal this time. But we'll bet on him," Earl added quickly. "We'd never bet against one of our own. But when the other cowboys and ranchers see that palomino stallion up close, see all those scar lines running down his shoulders and how big and strong he is, I think that the betting will run about even money."

"What did Jack say?"

"Said the hell with it all. Said he was a broncbuster and not a damn rodeo rider. He wants nothing to do with it."

"Then maybe we ought to forget the whole idea," Pete suggested.

"Can't. Mr. Tyson figures it ought to be a fine chance to show off Candy's palomino."

"You know Jack," Pete said, swallowing a mouthful of hot coffee. "Once he gets an idea in his head, he's as stubborn as a bulldog. I don't hardly think he will listen to me any more than he did to you."

"He might. All you got to do is get him to stall it for another hour or so. By then, the boss will be out here and he'll set the record straight. Jack is mighty testy this morning, but you'd be doing him a big favor."

"I'll do what I can," Pete said without enthusiasm, "but I don't want you fellas hanging around watching. Go about your business same as usual and just let me talk to him alone."

"Fine!" Earl said, looking greatly relieved. "This is Wednesday. We have four whole days to spread the word around about this coming Sunday. It's going to be the biggest event that ever took place on the Cross T!"

Pete stood and gazed out at the corral just in time to see Jack take out his rope and lean through the lower rails. He nodded his thanks to Peewee for saving him the coffee and then he started for the door.

"Best go easy," a cowboy warned. "Jack is on the prod this morning. And you know what a temper he has."

"Yeah," Pete answered, "I know."

When he reached the corral, Jack shouted, "Get your rope and my saddle and come on in here!"

"Why don't we wait up a while," Pete said. "The boys said that Mr. Tyson might have an idea about you riding the horse this next Sunday."

Jack didn't even look at him. He was watching the stallion, which now stood spraddle-legged at the far side of the corral, its eyes fastened on the hated rope. "You going to help me or not?"

Pete grabbed his own rope and slid through the rails. He moved up beside Jack who was careful to keep the heavy snubbing post between himself and the palomino. "I sure think it would be better to wait and make sure the boss . . ."

Jack pivoted and the palomino instantly saw the unguarded moment it had been waiting for. He lunged forward and, teeth bared, ears flattened, he came at Jack with murder in his eyes. It all happened so fast that if it hadn't been for the snubbing post, they both would have been stomped to mush.

"Look out!" Pete shouted, grabbing Jack and slamming them both forward into the post because there just wasn't time to reach the fence.

The stallion went by in a flash and by then they were both shaking out their ropes and separating for the throw. The horse went at Jack, so Pete caught its forelegs with the same loop he had used the day before and with the same results. He dug his heels into the soft earth, looped the rope around the back of his hips and braced himself for the impact.

The palomino hit the end of his rope less than a yard from Jack, whose loop settled over its head. The stallion's front legs were jerked out from under its body and it went down hard, only this time there was no rope around its hind feet and it was still able to rise and come at them. Jack used the snubbing post and with two quick twists the animal was tied and they were scooting out of its range—both dirty, out of breath and lucky to be in one piece.

"Here comes Lester with the boss and Miss Candy!" one of the mustangers yelled. "Better untie that stallion, Jack."

Jack shook his head, big fists knotted at his sides. He looked right at Sun Dancer and said apologetically, "I tried to do this the easy way, the honest and right way. But that fool owns you, not me, and so I got no choice but to walk away right now."

And that is just what he did.

"What the hell is going on out here?" Tyson demanded as he watched Jack stomp off toward the corral of mustang mares.

"Nothing," Pete said. "I roped Sun Dancer by mistake."

"The hell he did!" Lester swore. "That pigheaded broncbuster was going to ride him this morning, even after we told him you said not to."

Pete balled his fists but Tyson stepped in between them. "I want no trouble here," he warned. "Lester, you and your men mount up and go tend the cattle."

Lester jabbed a forefinger at Pete. "You better watch your manners."

"God damn it!" Tyson swore. "I said to ride out!"

The New Mexico cattle boss stomped away and when he was beyond earshot Tyson rumbled, "Why did Jack disobey my orders?"

"You'll have to ask him yourself," Pete answered in a testy voice. "But maybe he should have heard about the rodeo idea from you personally."

Tyson didn't like that, but he let it pass. "Start breaking the mares today. I've got a contract to fill by the end of next month with the Army brass out at Fort Churchill."

Pete nodded as the man turned away.

Candy started to follow her father back to the house, but then stopped and said to Pete, "Please don't get yourself forced into a fight with Lester Barron. He's too big and I don't want to see you get hurt."

"I won't back down from him or any man that calls me or Jack names. And I damn sure can't understand why your father hired him. Lester is trouble. First thing you know, he'll be telling your father what to do around here."

"I know. Father says he is the best with cattle he has ever seen. But I'm afraid of the man. I just try to tell myself that what is done is done."

Pete turned Sun Dancer free and headed toward the far corral where the mustang mares were penned. Jack was in no mood for conversation. Sensing that anything he said would be wrong, Pete did not wait for an invitation to get started as the mustangs nervously began to bunch up at the far side of the corral. His overhand loop sailed out and he caught a bay. He dug his heels into the dirt and let the horse drag him around until he got close enough to the snubbing post in the center to get two solid wraps. When the mare hit the end of the rope, she went straight up into the air and came down on her back. Before she could recover, Jack was running in to halter and blindfold her.

By the time she was struggling to her feet, he was back with Pete's scarred old saddle. The mare reared and the rope choked off her wind. She fought, but the harder she pulled the worse things got. That was the basic rule of breaking horses: When they fought, you had to make it hurt a little bit.

"Easy," Pete said with his smoothest voice. "Easy." He moved slowly back and forth, ready to leap away if the mare jumped at him with bared teeth or struck at him with a forefoot. Mares almost never did that, especially one that was preoccupied with breathing.

He placed his gloved hand on the taut rope. The mare plowed earth in a panic, but the tone of his voice never changed as he eased up the rope toward the horse. When he gently placed his hand on her muzzle, the animal again fought to escape, but by now she was beginning to realize that the rope was not going to release her, only choke when she fought. The hand moved up and slowly began to scratch the blazed face. Gradually, the mare began to settle. Her breath was tortured, but as she eased her weight up on the rope, she could breathe again.

Jack stepped forward and said, "You have a good touch

when you take your time. The thing to remember is that you just can't rush 'em, not ever. The half hour that you take today is going to save someone hours of grief later on. Be patient. Move and speak real nice and easy."

Pete kept on talking to the mare. When he began to rub the saddle blanket against her, the mare lurched back on her legs again. Pete waited a moment and then touched her again and within a very few minutes he was rubbing the blanket against her shoulders, then over her withers. Finally, he laid it across the mare's back.

"Now," he said quietly, "that wasn't so bad, was it?"

The mare stomped her hooves. She was bathed in nervous sweat, but her hide had stopped shivering. Pete hooked his left stirrup over his saddle horn so that it would be completely out of the way when it came time to cinch the mare tight. With one hand, he swung the forty-pound saddle onto the mare. She snorted and humped her back and kicked but he held the saddle in place and walked with her as she tried again to move away.

"Easy, easy," he crooned.

"This ought to be the one we break for Candy," Jack growled softly. "Good legs and a deep chest."

Pete wasn't listening because his concentration was fixed on the mare as he kicked out and caught the cinch ring with his pointed toe and pulled it under the mare's belly, then deftly stitched the latigo through and drew the cinch tight. Once more the mare fought but Pete kept hold of the latigo and halter rope and his voice never wavered. When the horse finally settled, he was ready to begin his ride.

Pete knew that mounting was the most dangerous part because there was an instant when the rider was totally off-balance with one leg planted in the stirrup and the other swinging through empty air. More broncbusters were hurt at that moment than in the saddle. Jack grabbed the mare's ear, twisting it hard enough to distract the animal, and Pete wasted no time swinging up and planting his boots in the stirrups. "Let 'er go!" Pete shouted, yanking the halter rope free with his gloved fist. "Yeehaw!"

The bay mare came unwound. Pete felt it uncorking up into the sky and he tried to make himself relax and not stiffen up too much because that only worsened the pounding. Instinct had told him that this was the strongest mare and the toughest bronc of the lot, and now she proved that he was right. This was a "sunfisher"—one of the toughest to ride because she kept twisting sideways as she went up into the air, trying to touch first one front shoulder to the earth, then the other.

The mare grunted every time she hit the earth, and just when Pete thought he had her rhythm figured, she dodged sideways quick as a cat and then began to spin. He spurred and quirted her hard, his own grunts coming in time with hers, but each time she landed, his face winced up as if he had been pounded in the kidneys. The bay kept spinning and he tried to drag her head up because it was getting too low. Jack had explained it a hundred times—keep their heads up and they can't get any power in their bucking, let their heads come down and they would beat you to death.

The mare snapped out of her spin and leaped forward. Two strides later, she planted all four hooves and erupted into the sky. She hit the earth like a pile driver and Pete gasped, his face ashen. He hung on until the mare ran out of fight and lifted her head, then began to crow-hop around the corral, each hop a little slower and less punishing, until she began to trot and he was plow-reining her this way and that.

He looked over at Jack as he dismounted. "One down and five to go," he managed to say as he led the mare back to the snubbing post, where he would unsaddle and turn her loose until it was time for another lesson tomorrow morning.

Jack nodded. "That was one hell of a fine ride, but I think I'll take the next one for you."

Pete did not argue.

CHAPTER FIVE

There are times in a man's life when he gets so damned tired that he can't sleep or even sit down and relax. His body feels like mush and his knees ache from holding his body upright, but his mind won't stop working. He feels restless, troubled and impatient with himself. That was how Pete felt that evening after dinner.

He and Jack had worked until dusk breaking the new mustang mares. Well, they weren't exactly broke, but each one of them had been ridden and that was the toughest part. Pete had never seen such uniformly splendid mares. Perhaps even more important, Sun Dancer's foals were obviously going to be superior horses.

Now, as Pete stood outside of Sun Dancer's moonlit corral and watched the stallion, he could not help thinking what a shame it was that the palomino had to be gelded. Sun Dancer was just the kind of stallion you wanted running free on the range. He was big and fast, straight-legged and intelligent. A lot of mustangs were stunted little animals that were tough, but not strong enough to work cattle or pull heavy wagons. That was why it was such a waste that this palomino would be taken off the range and not be allowed to upgrade the mustang blood. But that was how it always went: The very best were captured and the worst left to run wild. It didn't take a lot of intelligence to see that man was directly responsible for diluting the best qualities of wild horses.

"It's a damn shame," he said quietly, "that you can't just run another few years and breed us more of your kind of horses."

Sun Dancer stomped the earth impatiently as if to say he agreed.

"But maybe out there somewhere your sons are growing big and strong to take your place. Wouldn't surprise me." Pete knew very well that the stallion would drive his older sons away. "Maybe someday I'll ride over a ridge and see another horse like you and know that your blood carries on across this range."

"And then what will you do?" Maria asked quietly as she came to stand beside him. "Will you also rope, then castrate him for Candy so that she will have another plaything? You and that stallion are very fine, but she will be tired of you both within a year. This is sad, but the truth."

Pete groaned. "Maria, please, I've been breaking horses all day until I'm too damned tired to hardly think. I don't want to argue with you this evening."

She folded her arms over the rail beside him. "All right. But you looked lonesome out here by yourself. Are you afraid that Candy might see us together? If so, then I will leave."

"Stop it," he growled without any real anger. "I told you that I won't stop seeing you."

"I know but . . . we had better leave quickly!"

The tone of her voice warned him as much as her words. "What . . ."

"Lookee here!" Lester crowed to the man who trailed along beside him. "What do we have? Pete Sills, the Woman Killer, with Maria. Boy, some men have to beat 'em off with sticks, they're so damned handsome."

Pete started toward the man but Maria grabbed his arm. "No," she said. "Let us say goodnight. I want no trouble."

"Hell, let him run along! Me and you can cozy up together out in the brush somewhere," Lester said. "Maria, did you know that Pete has been romancing the boss's daughter? He's gonna sweet-talk himself into owning this whole damn outfit if someone don't derail his train."

The man beside him was named Ike and he laughed, but it was off-key and forced. "Maybe you oughta pull his switch right now, Les."

Pete wrenched his arm away from Maria. There was no chance he was going to walk away from this fight. His earlier mind-numbing weariness was forgotten as he stepped toward the man. Lester Barron probably thought Pete was going to try and talk his way out of this fight. Pete figured that gave him the chance to get in one solid first punch.

"Listen," he said, "I don't . . ." He never finished his sentence. Lester was so confident that his hands were still down by his sides and when Pete's overhand right smashed into his nose, the cow boss was caught flat-footed.

Pete felt Lester's nose break as he drove his fist behind the weight of his body. He saw Lester's shock and pain and then the man was crashing to the earth. Lester moaned, covered his face with his hands and brought them away to stare at his own blood.

"You dirty son of a bitch," he hissed. "I'm going to tear your head off for this."

Jack Kendall had taught Pete to avoid fights but when a man gave you no choice, you went at him hard and fast and you fought to win.

Pete waited until the man crawled up to one knee and then his boot whipped up and caught Lester under the chin. The man's head snapped backward and rolled sideways.

"Peter, look out!"

The light was good enough that he had no trouble seeing Ike's fist as it collided with his eye. Pete staggered. He felt

Maria catch him before he pushed her away and ducked a haymaker to drive his fist into Ike's belly. The man seemed to break in the middle and when his chin dipped, Pete tried to break his jaw with a chopping left hand. Ike dropped facedown, but before Pete could move he heard Maria cry out in pain.

Whirling around, he saw Lester hurl her against the corral. She groaned and sank to the earth and Pete could tell that she was injured. That filled him with an all-consuming anger. He came straight at Lester, tossing all guile and good sense to the winds.

For what seemed like forever, Pete stood toe to toe with Lester, trading his best punches with the bigger man. He had the satisfaction of seeing how his knuckles smashed flesh and when he took a punch he felt nothing. He could taste his own blood, feel a fire in his chest as he labored to stand and not give ground, hear the heavy grunts of pain that were torn from his own battered mouth as well as Lester's.

But despite everything, he was slowly giving ground to a bigger and stronger man. Pete screamed at himself to stand tall and not let this happen, but while his mind was strong, his body began to weaken under the thundering punches.

Suddenly Lester grabbed him by the throat. Pete heard Maria scream, then he felt himself being pinned against the pole corral. Lester began to smash his ribs and stomach. Pete tried to get off the rails but he was helpless. He lunged forward, wanting to grab the cow boss and hang on for a moment while his head cleared. Lester never gave him the chance. A vicious uppercut nearly took Pete's head off.

Maria was on her feet now. Her sounds were those of a wild animal in battle as she threw herself at Lester. Her fingernails raked his eyes and she beat at him in desperation.

Lester roared in anger and knocked her to the earth.

Pete shook his head and tried to find his legs. He wanted to raise his fists but his arms were too heavy.

Lester was half bent over, but now he straightened and his face was a mask of blood. His thick chest was heaving and his lips were smashed—but he wore a grin. "Say goodbye to your face, Woman Killer. I'm going to make it so ugly, dogs will howl to see you walk by."

A flood of icy fear washed through Pete and his mind was suddenly raindrop clear. He rolled sideways as Lester swung and the man's fist broke itself on a rail and he howled. Pete staggered forward and almost tripped over Maria, who was trying to get back to her feet and attack.

Pete straightened and saw the cow boss holding his broken right hand. He was aware of other men around him and that they were urging him on.

Jack Kendall leaned close and yelled in his face. "He's one-handed now, Pete. Take him! It's your turn. Don't let him get away with what he's done to you and Maria!"

Jack's words fired him with confidence and new strength seemed to flow into his legs and arms. Despite his ribs, Pete straightened tall, raised his fists, then went after the cow boss like a man bent on total destruction. He wanted to destroy this man, whip him so badly he would never bully or hurt anyone again. Lester tried to fight back, tried to block punches, but Pete was like a mighty desert whirlwind feeding on its own energy.

It was only when Lester crumpled to his knees and began to sob and beg for mercy that Pete realized the fight was over and Maria was trying to hold him back. It was then that he saw a pair of Lester's cowboys writhing on the ground with Jack towering over them.

Pete staggered away from Lester. He put his arm across Maria's shoulders and she half-carried him through the circle of cowboys and mustangers. Some tried to touch him.

Another said, "That was the greatest fight I ever saw in my life, Pete."

Pete knelt at the horse trough and ducked his numb face in the cold water. Then he rose again and they continued on toward the rose garden and Maria's door.

"Peter . . . my God, what happened to you!"

Maria stopped and gently turned Pete around so that he could see Candy, who now raised a lantern. When she saw him clearly, Candy's hand flew to her mouth.

Pete took a deep breath. He could not imagine how battered his face was, but Candy's reaction went a long way toward telling him. "Let's go," he said thick-voiced to Maria, "before I fall down and can't get up again."

"You'll always get up again, Peter." Then, taking one painful step at a time, they continued on inside.

He had spent a few minutes on Maria's couch while she and her mother tended to his injuries. Mostly, they had just bandaged ribs and cleaned up his face a little. Pete's lips were split and he had a few loose teeth, but otherwise he'd escaped the fight without serious injury. Maria wanted him to stay the night, but Peter declined, so she wanted to help him back to the bunkhouse.

"No, thanks. I'm in for enough teasin' without a woman half-carrying me to my bed."

Maria said, "Maybe you should not worry so much about appearances."

They stood in the rose garden and Pete could see that the bunkhouse was all lit up. It seemed possible there might still be more trouble between Lester's cowboys and the mustangers.

"I'd like to borrow a gun before I go over there," he said, trying hard not to alarm Maria.

"You think . . ."

"I don't know," he interrupted. "The only thing I'm sure

about is that I'm in no condition to fight anyone with my fists."

"We have an old Army pistol. It was my father's."

"Is it in firing order?"

She nodded and went to fetch it. When she returned, Pete knew that he had better hurry. He could hear the beginnings of an argument coming from the bunkhouse and it sounded angry.

"Thanks, Maria," he said, moving stiffly forward. "If you hadn't come to help, Lester would have beat the stuffing out of me."

"I'm not so sure of that. Be careful, Peter, and remember I love you!"

He nodded, feeling confusion. When he looked at her, he wanted to take her in his arms and hold her tight but then he thought of Candy and everything got confusing. Could a man love two women at the same time? He figured it was possible.

"I love you too, Maria. But I need to do a lot of hard thinking. I'll see you in the morning."

Pete inspected the gun as best he could in the moonlight and gathered it was a .36-caliber Navy Colt. A heavy and accurate weapon, primed and loaded.

When the voices grew louder, Pete decided he had better not go charging through the front door. Lester would be in a killing mood, and it was better to catch him by surprise.

The bunkhouse had two windows and Pete headed for the nearest one. The argument had escalated and he could hear Lester shouting threats and then the low, quiet but deadly voice of Jack Kendall in reply. Pete was surprised that Jack hadn't thrown the lot of the New Mexico hard cases out the door.

Surprised, that is, until he rubbed the window clean with his elbow enough to see that both Lester and Ike had guns trained on Jack's belly. The rest of Lester's men looked more worried than troublesome.

Pete stiffened. He had never shot at a man before, never even pointed a gun at one. This seemed a good time to start. He gripped the walnut handle of the pistol and moved around to the doorway. The bunkhouse had a small porch that squeaked, so he had to ease his weight down until he could move to the doorway.

Lester's voice quavered with fury. "Kendall, you and your friends are leaving right now, dead or alive. Which is it going to be?"

"I'll leave when I'm ready," Jack said, "and it won't be at gunpoint."

"I'm warning you!"

Pete stepped inside and said, "Drop the gun, Lester, or I'll blow your backbone through your belly button."

His little speech sounded silly but worked just fine. Lester stiffened and so did Ike. Lester's other cowboys made it clear they counted themselves neutral.

"I said to drop the gun!"

Ike dropped his gun as if it were a red-hot iron and Lester had no choice but to do the same. "I'll get even with you for this," he vowed. "I'll finish you before this is over, Woman Killer."

Jack Kendall struck like the head of a rattlesnake. His fist exploded against Lester's jaw and the man dropped without a sound.

"Ike, I want you and him off Cross T land before sunup or so help me I'll kill you both."

Jack's voice was almost conversational, which only made his warning all the more chilling. Ike nodded, grabbed Lester by the wrists and began to haul him out into the yard. They watched as Ike ran for their horses.

"What about us?" a cowboy asked. "We need the jobs."

"You chose sides a few minutes ago," Jack said, "and can stay."

A few minutes later, and with plenty of eager help from both the mustangers and cowboys, Ike had Lester tied across his saddle and they were trotting out of ranch headquarters.

"What's Mr. Tyson going to say when he gets back from Reno tomorrow?" one of the hands asked.

Pete shrugged as he limped toward his bunk, wanting nothing but the healing mercy of sleep.

"If he's smart, he'll say good riddance."

They turned out the lights then, but just before they did, Jack looked at him and winked with a crooked smile. "Where did you learn to fight so good for a skinny kid?"

Pete laughed, but that was a mistake because it made his ribs hurt. So he just grinned and stretched out on his bunk and closed his eyes. For a long time, he thought of Maria and how she tried to claw out Lester's eyes. And then he remembered Candy's beautiful face, and the shock it registered when she'd raised her lantern and seen him in the rose garden.

Pete was beginning to wonder if Jack was right again when he said that Maria was the girl that would stand by him in tough times. Win-or-lose times. It sure gave a fella something to think about.

By Saturday he was a new man. The swelling in his face had gone down and he could see fine with either eye. Best of all, he knew that his ribs were bruised and not broken. Because of the shape he'd been in, Jack had insisted he rest in bed and Pete hadn't argued much. While he recovered, Jack smoothed out the rough spots on the Sun Dancer mares.

But even though Pete was on his back, he could feel tension mounting as Sunday's rodeo approached. In the evenings Jack was withdrawn and seemed tired.

He was the first man in his bedroll at night and no longer the first out of it in the morning. This troubled Pete because the broncbuster had always been a wellspring of energy, a man constantly on the move.

Pete began to worry about his older friend. For the first time, he wondered what became of Jack and others like him when they were too old to keep breaking horses. In Jack's case, he was already far past the age when most broncbusters hunted up a new line of work. But the man's entire life revolved around horses and Pete couldn't imagine him doing anything else. Would Jack finally end up renting out livery horses in some stable to city folks? The very idea depressed Pete, for he understood that what happened to Jack might also reflect his own eventual fate. That meant he needed to start thinking about the future. He needed to watch and try to understand why a few men like Tyson succeeded in becoming important and having a spread of their own while others like Jack ended up with nothing but aching joints, wrinkles and empty pockets. Pete had seen them everywhere he went, men once strong now reduced to charity—he vowed it would not happen to him.

Late in the afternoon, most of the other cowboys rode over to Pine Grove or Rockland, where everyone had gold fever and claims were selling for nearly fifty dollars a running foot. In that kind of boomtown, gold or silver was all people talked about and Pete had no use for the cowboys who traded in their horses and saddles for a miner's outfit. Almost always, they ended up busted and afoot and came shuffling back to the ranches like beggars in hopes of returning to steady work and wages.

To Pete's way of thinking, when a man labored for nothing but the highest dollar, there could not be a hell of a lot of pride in him, and whatever job he did to earn his wages would be half-baked anyway. But if you were like Peewee the cook and couldn't physically do the work you loved anymore, well, that was another matter entirely. The country was full of old-time bronc fighters and cowboys tending bars, cooking and pitching hay in livery stables and they had nothing to be ashamed about when it was the best they could get.

Saturday evening found Pete hanging around the corrals, just killing time.

"Pete? What are you thinking?"

He was leaning on the corral fence watching the stallion, thinking about how that magnificent animal must have lost a hundred pounds this week because of fretting over his captivity.

He turned and saw Candy standing in the dim light. "I was thinking of Jack Kendall and what's going to happen to him after he leaves."

His answer seemed to disappoint her. "He'll be better off. He should have left a long time ago, when Mother died."

"Did you know about that?"

"Of course. Didn't everyone?"

"Yeah, I guess they did at that. In a way, I guess it's lucky for you that your mother married your father instead of Jack."

"If Jack had married Mother, he might have owned this ranch instead of my father. Women make men do things they wouldn't do otherwise."

Pete had never thought of it that way. "I suppose." Pete toed the earth. "I plan to make something of myself. I mean . . . well, have a place of my own like this."

"You can do whatever you want. Even go to school and become a doctor or a lawyer if you wanted."

"I wouldn't like that. My talent," he said, not wanting to

sound at all like a braggart, "is with horses, not books and figures."

"Can you read or write?"

"Sure!" Pete was offended. "I can do both; I just don't like to."

"Mr. Lawson once wrote me poetry," Candy said, watching him closely.

"Isn't he that fat assistant banker?"

She placed her hands on her shapely hips and sounded exasperated. "He may be a little overweight but he has a poet's soul—you, on the other hand, have the soul of a . . . a Philistine!"

"A what?"

"Never mind." She took a deep breath and looked through the rails at the mustang. "Do you think Jack can ride him?"

"We'll find out tomorrow."

"I almost hope that he can't, so that you get the chance to show everyone how good you really are. It is not that I want to see Jack hurt, but it's your time—his has passed."

The way she said that made Pete stiffen a little because time seemed to him to belong to everyone as long as they were alive. The idea that your time was up at only forty-two years of age did not seem quite right.

She reached up and kissed him full on the mouth and before he could reach for her, she was backing away, saying, "I'm glad your face is about normal. You looked terrible on Thursday!"

He hooked a bootheel over the bottom rail, thinking how this girl was always jumping out of reach after one good kiss. "Goodnight, Candy."

"Goodnight and good luck tomorrow. It's your turn."

Maybe and maybe not, he thought, watching her walk back to the ranch house and admiring her form every step of the way. He wanted to put on a show tomorrow, but not if that meant seeing Jack Kendall get hurt.

On Sunday morning he headed across the ranch yard for Sun Dancer's corral, one side of which was draped with a canvas tarp to block the stallion from the sight of his mares in the hope of settling him down. When Pete rounded the tarp, he almost collided with Jack, who was already there, standing alone, smoking a cigarette and concentrating on the palomino. It was an awkward moment and Pete was about to swing away when Jack's voice stopped him in his tracks.

"If this stud beats me, you watch how he does it and that will be your edge. Study him close and you'll have a better chance."

Jack stuck out his thick, work-stiffened hand. "Good luck," he said in a voice that sounded husky. "This one or the next, you're going to be great. I wish you the best on Cross T when I'm gone."

Pete took the powerful hand and shook it hard. "I owe you plenty," he managed to say. "I'll miss having you around."

"Same here, but ride or fall, I'm leaving tomorrow."

Pete nodded. In the early morning light, he noticed again how old and tired Jack looked and how the creases in his face seemed deeper than he had remembered.

CHAPTER SIX

They began to trickle in from the mining and ranching communities at seven o'clock and they kept rolling in all morning. By eleven, the barbecue pit was already down to coals and the cowboys were enjoying a cask of Tyson's California red wine and taking turns cranking a side of beef over the coals while trying to look good for the ladies. Some cowboys from the nearby ranches brought guitars and fiddles and were playing for the growing crowds but no one was ready to dance yet. Overhead, the clouds were big and lumbering. Miles to the north, they could hear thunder like distant cannon and the sky was dark and threatening. To Pete, it looked as if there might be rain before evening, but by that time no one would care.

Whenever the sun was covered by clouds, the air cooled and Pete thought of how it would give Maria and her mother some relief in the steamy kitchen where they worked feverishly to make potato salad, boil corn and keep their fresh pies from burning.

Candy Tyson was everywhere, laughing and smiling, aware that the eyes of every young man on the ranch were following her movements with longing and desire. Men crowded near her. These were the sons of other ranchers or of prominent townspeople, those with bright and profitable futures.

Shortly before noon, Pete saw Maria begin to carry out trays of food and she was immediately surrounded by cowboys falling all over themselves with eagerness to help. Maria smiled and let them compete for her attention. Her dark eyes happened to find his own and, for a moment, lock. Then she laughed softly and he could almost read her thoughts telling him that she could easily find another man who would gladly love and marry a poor girl of mixed blood.

Pete strolled on until he heard Candy's laughter. She was completely surrounded by a group talking animatedly about things to see in San Francisco, a city he had never visited. One of the young men was dressed in a handsome suit and was telling her about a famous oceanside restaurant. Candy seemed entranced.

Pete left the gathering of fine, prosperous young men and women whose custom-tailored suits and dresses made his new trousers and Sunday shirt look commonplace. He tried to push down the idea that nothing he could ever do would elevate him into contention for the boss's daughter. Next to the young and well-to-do bachelors surrounding her, he felt as common as a rusty old horseshoe.

But when he passed a group of cowboys and heard them arguing over whether the palomino stallion could be ridden by the great Jack Kendall, Pete's spirits lifted. Maybe he was outclassed by better-educated and richer young men, but as he looked around at the cowboys and even some other damned good broncbusters and mustangers, he knew that not one of them could stick a wild horse better.

Pete sauntered out of the ranch yard and into the valley to join a large crowd of men who were betting furiously over an upcoming race between a Paiute's mustang and a long-legged buckskin that looked as if it could cover twenty feet at a stride.

"You betting, Pete?"

"What's the odds?"

"Three to one. Buckskin is favored."

"How far are they running?"

The man pointed it out and Pete guessed the track was only about three hundred yards long, which favored the much shorter coupled mustang. He studied both horses. The mustang couldn't have weighed over seven hundred pounds. It had a big jughead and a thin, pinched-looking U-neck. Its coat was dull and its mane and tail full of sticker-balls. But its legs were clean and straight and it had a fire in its eyes, so Pete bet on it because he liked the odds.

The starter fired a gun and the mustang took off as if a Chinese rocket had been shoved underneath its tail. Its rider flattened on its shaggy little back, and before the man on the buckskin could get his long-legged horse untracked, the mustang had a four-horse lead. Everyone was shouting and yelling and still figuring the buckskin would plow the mustang under. But it never did. The smaller horse laid back its ears and sailed across the grass, not increasing its lead, but not losing a foot of it either until the very last few strides when the buckskin finally seemed to wake up and realize it was being humiliated.

Pete won fifteen dollars. Ordinarily, that would have called for a drink, but today he couldn't have kept one down because his stomach was churning. Back at the stud corral, he saw Jack Kendall opening the gate and hauling his Colorado saddle inside to Sun Dancer, who was already lashed to the heavy snubbing post.

One look told Pete that the old broncbuster had waited long enough. He was going to climb on Sun Dancer, and get the show over with so that he too could eat and drink and have a good farewell party. Pete didn't blame him one damned bit.

It took some doing for Jack to get the palomino saddled, even with Pete's help. All the while they worked together,

Jack was silent and grim; he spoke no calming words to the mustang and Pete guessed it was because the man had decided this was going to be an all-out war and whichever of them could inflict the most pain first was going to be the winner.

When the cinch was pulled tight, the stallion fought so hard it reared over backward and almost choked to death before they could get it up again. Jack cussed a blue streak because his beloved Colorado saddle had its horn snapped off at the fork.

They had to change saddles and let the stallion settle down a few minutes. While they waited, Pete thought about how that saddle had been mighty special to Jack for a lot of rough years. Jack had ordered it custom-made by Gallup and Frazier out of Pueblo, Colorado, a few years ago. The saddle horn had been tall and slender with a little curve to it and the horn was small instead of fat and squatty like those preferred by the Mexican and California ropers. The fork had prominent and rounded swells so that a broncbuster could get his knees under it and hang on tight. Coupled with a five-inch-high cantle, cowboys had dubbed Jack's saddle a "form-fitter"—you got fitted inside it with a shoehorn and the only way a bronc had a chance to loosen you was to roll over and pry you off his back with a screwdriver.

As they resaddled the palomino, Pete realized that the broncbuster hadn't bothered to dress up fancy like everyone else. Jack was dressed in his faded Levi's and rough work shirt, just like any other working day. His scarred and battered chaps had long since lost their shiny conchas and his Stetson was shapeless and sweat-stained without so much as a nice braided hatband. Jack's old boots were mashed down flat at the toes and scuffed so bad the leather appeared to be rough side out. Compared to everyone else on the Cross T, he looked downright shabby and that was all the more unusual, considering he was the top half of today's main attraction.

But none of the cowboys who understood Jack and really appreciated what was about to happen thought anything the less for his appearance. They climbed up on the top rails to spit and chew and there wasn't one of them who would have traded his place, not even for a kiss from Candy or Maria.

Jack pulled his ugly hat down over his eyes and in a low, strained voice said, "Pete, when I get into the saddle, you cut him free. Got your jackknife?"

"Sure," Pete said, feeling his own stomach knot almost as bad as if he were making this ride himself.

"You watch him close. See how he goes. I got a feeling I'll only be able to climb on him once, so I'm going to give him hell from the first buck to the last."

Pete swallowed. "I hope you ride him, Jack."

He smiled broadly and took a deep, deep breath. "So do I."

And then he stepped into the saddle as fluid as a big cat as Pete slashed ropes until the stallion broke free. It stood trembling with fury until Jack reached down and tore away the blindfold, then its head snaked back and forth and it suddenly erupted straight up on its hind legs and squealed as it clawed for the sky. For a moment, it tottered, and just when it looked as if things were going to come out right, it arched its back and went over backward. Women screamed and cowboys stopped chewing as Jack Kendall kicked out of the saddle and dropped lightly to the earth. The stud crashed over and twisted, then shook its head clear and scrambled up as Jack vaulted back into the saddle.

The cowboys cheered and so did the women, but they fell silent as the stud began to grunt and twist and buck so viciously that it was apparent to everyone that no man could long take that punishment.

Pete classified Sun Dancer as a "high-roller," a horse that throws himself straight up and then comes down stiff-legged. He knew that this was the worst possible kind for Jack because he would jar his insides loose, insides that had seen too many years of this kind of violent wrenching. Over and over, Sun Dancer threw himself up at the sky only to land stiff-legged, and each time he did, Jack's face lost more color. The spectators became grim-faced and some of the cowboys chewed faster and shook their heads as Jack fought to keep his own head from snapping back and forth. He spurred hard, tried to use his quirt, tried to use every inch of his legs to hang on and outlast the powerful mustang.

Now the stallion began to swap ends back and forth, and when Jack still hung on, it seemed to realize it could not get rid of the man by bucking. Sun Dancer pulled the last desperate card from his deck as he lunged straight for the snubbing post. Pete yelled and it seemed as if Jack could not raise his head to see the onrushing danger. The stud was going to crush Jack's leg against the post and rip him free.

When the palomino hit the post, Pete heard Jack scream in agony and then slump over in the saddle, but by then Pete was already inside the corral and running to catch his friend and pull him out of danger before the stallion stomped him to death.

A dozen hands pulled the broncbuster through the rails and when they laid him out on the ground, Jack was still conscious. He stared up at Pete and the tight circle of grim-faced cowboys and tried to smile. "That damned horse is yours to finish now that I've smoothed off his rough edges."

It was a joke, but nobody felt like laughing, least of all Pete.

Jack gripped his wrist hard. "Don't get fancy. You seen how he goes?"

Pete nodded. "I saw enough."

"He's a killer," one of the men said with awe in his voice. "Smart thing to do is to shoot that stallion before someone else gets hurt."

Jack's eyes had closed, but now they snapped open. "Nobody," he grated, "shoots that stud. He didn't ask for what he's getting. All he wanted was to breed good horseflesh and be left to run free. If Pete can't break him to ride, then he deserves to be turned loose!"

Tyson knelt down beside his old mustanging friend. He glanced at the injured leg and said to Pete, "Why don't we turn him loose. Candy is pretty upset. She doesn't want anyone else to get hurt and she thinks Sun Dancer can't be ridden."

Pete stood up and pulled down his hat so it rested on his eyebrows and his ears. He looked down at Jack Kendall and completely ignored his boss. "I'll give him a little hell of my own."

The men parted as he trudged back to the corral. When he stepped through the rails, two cowboys had already roped Sun Dancer and the stud was watching him, eyes red and treacherous.

Pete tightened his spurs as he glanced at Candy and Maria. Candy looked excited, but Maria looked just plain worried. Her hands were clasped together and he realized she was praying for him. Pete appreciated that; he guessed he could use all the help he could get.

Sun Dancer's powerful neck snaked back and forth and he rolled his eyes. Pete took a deep breath and started toward the horse, wiping his sweaty palms on his pants and discovering that his throat was too dry to even swallow.

For the very first time in his young, hell-bent-for-leather existence, Pete knew the meaning of pure fear.

Sun Dancer waited for him to put his foot into the stirrup and swing his leg over the cantle and that's when he uncorked. Pete was caught off-balance and slingshotted halfway across the corral to crash against the rails. Picking himself off the ground, he shook his head and rolled his shoulders, making sure that every limb still worked. Satisfied they did, he started back toward the stallion, grateful that both mounted cowboys had been sharp enough not to ease up on their stretched ropes.

"Pete," Tyson called worriedly, "give it up!"

"Never was a horse couldn't be rode," Pete growled to himself. This was a simple matter of honor now. The horse had fought and done what it had to do to rid itself of something on its back, something just like a mountain lion that had clawed the devil out of it years ago. Pete ignored the crowd, the shouted suggestions from the older cowboys and the encouragements from the younger ones. This was between him and Sun Dancer and everyone and everything faded away into the background.

He moved swiftly toward the horse and grabbed the bucking rope. This time, instead of planting his foot in the stirrup, he grabbed the saddle horn and vaulted up. It was quite a feat, considering the height and his injured ribs, but he landed smoothly and found both stirrups as if his boots had eyes in their pointed toes.

There was a rawhide quirt around his right wrist and spurs on his boots and he used them hard now as the ropers pitched their lariats away. The stud rocked back on its haunches and launched itself toward the sky. Pete was ready because the palomino had made exactly the same initial move with Jack. He rode it through a series of jarring, head-whipping, pile-driving bucks until the stud reared up and came over backward once again. Pete kicked out of the stirrups and lit on his feet. He dodged a bite and leaped back in the saddle as the animal clambered to its feet.

Sun Dancer squealed more in anger than in pain and

began to buck around and around in circles. When it suddenly changed directions, Pete was left hanging out like wash on the line but he somehow managed to recover his seat. The contest grew even more violent. He and the stud hurt each other with every buck. His spurs raked hide and hair, and every time the animal came down, Pete's jaw slammed against his chest and he grunted in agony as his ribs seemed to collapse on him.

He could hear blood pounding in his ears over the roar of the spectators. His breath came hard and the stud was gasping too. Again, the animal spun and Pete grabbed for the saddle horn. Miraculously, the animal surged right back under him and he punished it harder with the quirt and spurs.

His nose bled and his left arm lost its strength and Pete could no longer hold the stud's head up. But Sun Dancer's strength was also fading. His bucking slowed and he seemed to be using the last of his dwindling reserves to make each buck more savage than the last. As they went around and around in a red haze of pain, Pete saw streaks of color and faces, a watery collage of yelling and cheering humanity.

The stud turned and jolted into a run straight for the snubbing post. The cheers turned to warning screams and Pete barely managed to get his head up and see the onrushing danger. He kicked his leg high and Sun Dancer crashed into the post, grunting as the empty stirrup punched into its bloodied and spur-raked flanks. The palomino staggered, almost fell. Pete slashed it hard across the rump.

The mustang groaned and shuddered to a standstill. Pete raised his eyes and realized he was facing Candy and Maria. He wiped blood from his nose and smiled, then doffed his hat for the crowd and they loved it. Older men nodded with silent admiration and younger ones shouted their appreciation. Candy blew him a kiss right in front of her father.

Maria wiped her eyes dry and returned to the ranch kitchen.

Pete toppled from the saddle and had to be helped out of the corral. Mr. Tyson pumped his hand and pounded his back. "That was one of the greatest rides I ever seen in my life!" he boomed loud enough for everyone to hear. "Even Jack Kendall couldn't have done it better when he was your age."

Pete lifted his chin. "Jack is still the best."

"Sure he was! But you are now!"

Candy took his arm. "We had better get you cleaned up and presentable."

"For what?"

Candy smiled. "You'll see."

An hour later he was dressed in a fancy silk shirt that Hugh Tyson insisted he keep. Pete raised a glass of imported champagne and returned the toast of his boss, who bellowed, "I am giving this fine young broncbuster a hundred dollars for riding that stallion. He proves without a doubt that the Cross T has always had the top broncbuster in western Nevada on its payroll. Pete, I'm sure you can use the money; you damned sure earned it."

He held the money out and Pete started to take it but then pulled back his hand. Tyson's grin faded and he said, "Go ahead, I want you to have it."

"Nope," he decided firmly. "I figure topping a horse like Sun Dancer was an honor and just part of my job. I can't take it, sir."

Tyson blinked and stared at him. Slowly, he returned the crisp, new bills to his wallet and said, "I respect you for that. It's exactly what Jack Kendall said when I mentioned a bonus."

Pete raised his own glass and turned toward the bunkhouse where Jack lay in pain. "To Jack Kendall," he said in a voice so quiet that everyone had to strain to listen. "He's the man that taught me everything I know about mustanging and breaking wild horses. And about honor and doing what you believe is right."

There was an embarrassed silence that lasted until the Cross T cowboys and mustangers began to clap their hands and then everyone joined in a thundering ovation. Pete blushed with pride and embarrassment. But once again, he felt the eyes of both Candy and Maria and he sure wondered what they were thinking.

It was past midnight and they had built a huge bonfire to light their dancing. Pete had drunk enough wine to dull the constant throbbing of his ribs. It was a wonderful party, the finest night of his life. He danced with Candy at every opportunity and cut in a few times as if it were his right. In between dances, he even grew bold enough to join far more successful men in a lively discussion. He might have avoided that debate, but it centered on someone's outrageous plan to rid the country of mustangs because they competed with increasing numbers of cattle for water and grass. During the dry years, cattle might starve or die of thirst while the wily stallions filled their worthless bellies and their bands flourished.

Pete strongly disagreed with the idea that the wild horse ought to be eradicated because there was strong and growing need for sound, green-broke mustangs. Those not intelligent or fast enough to be saddle horses were sent to the big Eastern cities where they would pull wagons, cabs and cable cars. Sadly, many would be overworked on hard street surfaces until their tendons and fragile leg bones failed and they were sold to the rendering plants.

The Army took many to the battlefield and others only slightly more fortunate wound up behind a farmer's plow or pulling his wagons. The West needed building and mules were often too expensive to buy and feed. A small sodbuster quickly realized that the hardy mustangs could live on practically nothing and were amazingly strong for their size.

Listening to the cattlemen, Pete realized for the first time how deeply the mustang was resented. Figuring his opinion was as good as theirs, he said, "Mustangs have their place on this range. Everyone needs good horses."

"Then I say they should breed their own," a rancher snapped.

Another added, "Best way is just to kill all the studs and then the mares will be leaderless and you can catch 'em easy."

"No studs, no foals," Pete said, trying hard not to lose his temper. "Besides, it's the best ones like Sun Dancer that breed good horses."

The young man who had earlier that afternoon been the center of Candy's attention argued, "If that's the way you feel, then why did you even agree to help catch him?"

He glanced at Candy. "Because I think a very special woman should have a very special horse, don't you?"

The man blushed and tossed down his drink before moving stiffly away.

"Thank you," Candy said, taking his arm to lead him away. "I need to ask you something about that animal, but we have to look at him first."

"It's dark out there," her father complained.

This caused an outburst of laughter and Pete heard one rancher say, "Better watch that young bronc stomper of yours, Hugh, or he'll break your daughter along with your horses."

Tyson laughed nervously.

Pete and Candy stood beside the pole corral away from the others and watched Sun Dancer between the rails.

"What'd you want to know about him?" Pete asked.

"What I really want to know is why you turned my father's hundred dollars down."

The question caught him by surprise. He'd assumed she would understand that it was a matter of professional pride.

"You know," she continued, "my father started the Cross T Ranch on less than one hundred dollars cash. Jack Kendall will tell you that. I believe it can still be done if a man is tough and smart. There's no question that you're tough, but when you turned down the money, I had to wonder if you're very smart?"

Pete took a deep breath. "Well, I believe in getting ahead. I think a man should do whatever is most profitable."

"Good!" She smiled. "And what would you say if I told you that my father has decided to go even bigger into cattle ranching. Prices are high and going higher every day. He intends to hire another cattle boss to replace Lester."

Pete gripped the rail. Cross T was already overstocked and the news that Tyson intended to buy even more cattle troubled him mightily. "This is a mustanging outfit, damn it! Horses are what pays our rent."

"Father thinks that when the war ends, the market for horses will die. The Union is winning; Father thinks the war is nearly over."

"But after the war there will be an even greater need for horses! Men will return to the land, plant crops, buy buggies and wagons. What your father thinks just doesn't make good sense."

"Peter? Couldn't you at least think about asking my father if you could handle the cattle? You know enough that . . ."

"No," he almost shouted. "I'm a mustanger and a broncbuster. I'm the best at what I do and there are already enough men who can punch cattle."

She was silent a long time. "Pete, you're a wonderful rider, but that can't last forever. You have to think ahead."

"I have."

She was getting angry. "To what! Becoming old and broken like Jack Kendall with nothing but a saddle and a bagful of memories? Did you see the look on his face when he couldn't ride Sun Dancer? Do you want that to happen to you!"

Pete swallowed. He knew what she was saying. Jack had looked a hundred years old and it wasn't because of the pain in his leg. "Candy, I don't know how to put it any other way except to tell you that I love horses and mustanging. They're my life. I can't change that."

"And I can't change the fact that I want a forward-looking man. One like Father who wants to amount to something. Don't throw everything away."

He shook his head. The anger suddenly washed out of him. "Let's not fight, Candy. I've got big plans, but they have to involve horses, not cattle. Give me a chance."

She threw her arms around his neck. "I love you. You have very special qualities. I'm sure you're going to see things differently and you must, because I won't marry someone who is going to fail."

He wanted to tell her that he had no intention of failing. Mustanging had built Cross T and would continue to earn Tyson big profits for years to come. Pete believed that if men left the top stallions like Sun Dancer to run free and breed superior horses, mustangs would always be prized.

"Pete?" Candy stepped back, looking deeply troubled. "I have to ask you this. What if my father ever decided to shoot all the stallions and foals?"

"But why?"

"To increase the feed for our cattle."

Pete took a deep breath and let it out slowly. The idea of

shooting wild horses just because they competed for graze turned his stomach. "Would he do that?"

"I don't know," she said in a hopeless voice. "My father has changed so much. All I can tell you is that he was seriously considering the idea before Lester went away. Lester had Father convinced that if we eliminated all the mustangs, Cross T could stock another several thousand cattle. Other ranchers are talking about it too. That's one of the reasons I wanted Sun Dancer so badly. I kept thinking someone might kill him."

Pete touched her cheek. Now he understood her better. He wished he could tell her that everything would be fine, but that wasn't possible.

"Pete," she said with growing urgency, "if my father decides to do that, what . . ."

"I just couldn't stand by and let it happen."

"But you couldn't stop him!"

Pete chose his next words very deliberately. "I know you love your father, Candy, but if he ever begins to slaughter mustangs, I'll start packing an extra gun."

She whirled and he stood immobile. She had told him that he had to choose between her and mustanging. He'd made it equally clear that she might have to choose between him and her father.

Pete slammed his fist against the top rail of the corral. Maybe everything would work out fine between him and Candy, but right now that seemed damned unlikely.

CHAPTER SEVEN

The doctor from Yerington climbed into his buggy and Pete handed his medical bag up to him. "Jack needs to stay off that leg for a month so the bone will mend straight. Make sure he follows my orders."

"Jack doesn't listen to anybody and he never has, Doc."

The man frowned. "Isn't that the damned truth. Well, at least try to keep him on crutches and off any horse, will you?"

"I'll do my best. Sure you won't stay for breakfast? Peewee is cooking biscuits."

"Can't stay. Got a lot of calls to make today, Pete. Thanks anyway."

He watched the doctor drive away and then he headed for the corral. Last evening Tyson had ordered him to castrate Sun Dancer. That sort of surprised him because, even though he had assisted Jack dozens of times, he had never actually castrated a stud by himself.

It took the next two hours to rope and drop Sun Dancer. They tied his forelegs and then made a yoke around his neck. Next, they buckled a pair of strong leather hobbles on the rear pasterns, threaded a rope through the neck yoke and pulled both rear legs sharply forward, exposing the stallion's testicles, with the powerful hind legs locked beside his ribs. Jack had always insisted on washing the testicles with lye and soap and this stallion did not enjoy the sensation.

"Got your knife?" Jack asked casually as he leaned his

crutches up against the corral fence and came hopping over on one leg to join him.

"You should be in bed resting! Hell, Jack, the dust from the doctor's buggy is still hanging in the air."

"Get out your knife and it had best be sharp. This horse is going to suffer enough as it is with me teaching you how to operate."

Pete dug out his knife. Like most every cowboy he knew, he kept it ground razor-sharp. "It's a damn shame, isn't it," Pete said as he studied the horse.

"It's a waste for sure," Jack agreed. "If I had the say-so, he'd be turned loose, but he's Tyson's horse."

Pete lit a match over the blade of his knife because Jack felt that doing so cauterized the wound and diminished the bleeding. He reached out and hefted the testicles and the stallion struggled fiercely but was helpless. "How deep?"

"Pretty deep," Jack said. "Last thing you want to do is have to saw your blade back and forth. Cut him fast and deep and then pull 'em out."

Pete took a deep breath. He wished that they had called the damn veterinarian. They would have, except that old Jack had insisted that someday he might have to do it out on the range without help and it was best to learn now, rather than later.

"Go on!" Jack snapped. "Waitin' doesn't make it any easier. You know where to cut."

Steeling himself, Pete jabbed the point of the blade in deep and then sliced a line almost four inches long. The stud went crazy but Pete hardly noticed how its body rocked in pain. He reached into the bloody scrotum and grabbed the mass of testicle and sliced it from its cords just as if it was a grape off the vine.

While the stallion fought helplessly, Jack pitched him a little can of Dr. Crockett's Horse Salve, which Pete applied to the deflated scrotum, rubbing it around inside, then over the oozing incision.

"The second one is easier on both of you," Jack said drily. "Thing to remember is that a stud doesn't live very long. Either some rancher will shoot him on sight for stealing his good mares, or a younger and stronger stud will come along and cripple him, run him off to die alone. A gelded riding horse will survive about twice as many years."

"But he won't have half the fun," Pete said grimly as he removed the second testicle. Jack had been right about this part being quicker; the palomino was either in shock from pain or had given up, knowing that his life was going to take on a whole new outlook. In either event, he hardly fought at all.

"Fun, huh?" Jack scratched his head. "Maybe so, but this horse will never kill himself over the opposite sex again. All he will care about, if you did your job right, is just to graze and do as little work as he can. He'll be able to see truths that he couldn't because of what you just removed. He'll act a lot smarter, take life a lot easier and probably be just as happy, all things considered."

Pete didn't buy a word of it as he finished applying the salve, then picked up the egg-sized testicles and flung them to the waiting ranch dogs, who fought over them like crazy. He nodded to Jack, who silently headed back to the bunkhouse.

Once Jack was out of the corral, Pete untied the mustang, but the poor horse just lay there on his side groaning. Watching it suffer affected Pete strongly. Life was a tough road for man or beast and though a lot of studs had benefited from being gelded and broken to a saddle or harness, Pete was afraid Sun Dancer might not be one of them.

When he turned to walk away, he almost ran headlong

into Candy. She must have read something of his thoughts because she took his arm. "I guess it wasn't easy for you."

"It's my job now. No sense in paying a veterinarian for what I should be doing."

"How soon will you start riding him?"

He blinked, twisted around and glanced at the animal lying on its side. "Well . . . I thought I'd give him a few days to recover."

"My father said that the best time to work him is right away." Her eyes slid away from his. "He'll be in such pain that he won't be able to buck. By the time the pain and swelling are gone, he'll be as gentle as a pony!"

"I see," he told her quietly.

"I knew you would. You're smart, Pete. We'll both be interested to know how you and Sun Dancer get along on your ride this afternoon."

His mouth crimped with anger. However, before he could think of anything to say, she turned and was gone. Pete watched her sashay off, but this time he was not in an admiring frame of mind and the idea occurred to him that maybe she was not the woman for him after all. She obviously did not care if Sun Dancer started bleeding heavily or how much pain the animal might suffer from being ridden so quickly after the operation.

He was in a black mood as he rode the gelding that same afternoon and Sun Dancer did suffer too much pain to offer him a fight. Candy returned and was delighted and her father seemed pleased as the horse settled down with each passing day of work. There was no infection and no bleeding and the animal was smart and chose to learn rather than battle. Within a week, Pete had the gelding broken to ride and after two more weeks it would rein decently, stop, back up and stand still while being mounted and dismounted. The big palomino worked so easily that sometimes Pete had the feeling the animal was saving itself for the opportunity to explode and kill him if he became unwary. When he asked Jack about that, the broncbuster told him that you could never be quite sure about a wild horse who had run free with his own band of mares for so long. Sometimes they lay in wait like a live bullet in a cowboy's campfire.

Late one afternoon, Maria came to see him alone for the first time since the big celebration at the Cross T. "We must talk tonight," she told him.

"What's wrong with right now?"

"No, what I have to say is to be said in private."

They met in the moonlit valley and Pete's breath caught in his throat and he whistled in soft admiration, for she was wearing a new dress and brushed her long black hair until it gleamed in the starlight. She had even braided some small white rosebuds into her hair and the effect was stunning.

Pete did not quite know what to say.

Finally, Maria could stand it no more. She turned to him and with a voice almost breaking, said, "I only want to know this. Do you love her—or her father's money?"

The question caught him totally off guard. Now that she had asked, he wondered why he had never thought of Candy in terms of love. Passion, yes. Money, power and success, of course. Though he intended to make his own successes in life, marrying Candy would guarantee all of those things.

"Tell me the answer to that question!" Maria cried. "If you truly love her, I will pray for your happiness. But if you prefer her for her father's money, then you should be ashamed."

"I don't know if I love her or not," he admitted. "And as for her father, I think likely I will soon fight him over this range. But I have dreams, Maria. Big dreams. I don't want to end up like Jack Kendall, old before my time and wondering where I'll find my next job."

"He will be fine! Señor Kendall is strong and good in his heart."

"I guess it sounds selfish and shallow, but I want to have money."

"Money is nice," she said after a long pause. "I would like some money too. God knows that my poor mother and I have never had anything since my father deserted us. But we do not complain."

"Of course you don't, I . . ."

Maria placed her hands on his shoulders. She looked down at the dress she had made herself. "I would also like to have money. I would buy a couple of new dresses, one right out of the store window. And a horse. I have always wanted a horse of my very own. We could go riding together."

He had to smile. "I already do enough riding."

"I could help you catch wild horses, no? You could teach me all about the mustangs. Wouldn't that be wonderful?"

She looked so excited by the idea that he grinned and nodded his head.

She reached up on her toes and kissed him. He willed himself not to hold her and when she stepped back, Maria's joy was gone and she swallowed with disappointment. "I understand, Peter. She still has you under her power right now. She has done it to many others, but it never lasts. She will use you and then throw you away when she is finished."

"No," he said woodenly. "You don't understand."

"It is you who do not understand. But I tell you this; I may take you back. No promises, but I may."

"Thank you," he said, feeling a little humbled and foolish.

"You are very welcome," she replied formally. "Now, goodnight."

After she had left, Pete sat down on the grass and stared up at the constellations, trying to remember some of their names. He struggled to figure out what it was that he really wanted in life. He did want money and a place of his own, but most of all, he figured that he wanted a good woman who understood his love of mustanging and horses.

Maria or Candy? The hell of it was, he couldn't have them both.

He had ridden Sun Dancer all that morning, worked it hard and let it run for miles across the long, dry valleys, testing its speed. Pete had never ridden an animal that even remotely compared to this palomino. The big horse seemed to devour the land in huge bounding strides. Ears flat to its head, neck straight out and low to the ground, the sensation of being on its back was exhilarating.

Pete wished Jack could see how fast the animal ran under saddle. But the old broncbuster was still on crutches. And lately, he seemed to have drawn into himself. He hadn't become unfriendly, but it was as if he had already left the Cross T Ranch. His mind had gone ahead and expected his body to follow when it healed. About the only thing that Jack seemed interested in was the palomino. Jack would make it a point to struggle out to the corral early every morning to watch Sun Dancer being trained and exercised. But he never offered any suggestions, never so much as hinted he might have ideas on how to make that horse the best that it could be.

It had taken a while for Pete and the others to adjust to the change in Jack's temperament. For years cowboys and mustangers alike had come to Jack for advice on horses. But now he always referred their questions to Pete. Sometimes the cowboys asked Pete, but more often, they just walked away. This bothered him until he realized that just because he had taken Jack's place, it didn't mean that he could fill his boots. That would take years, and Pete no longer thought he would stay that long on the Cross T. He tried to put his mind to other things, but he kept thinking about how Tyson had almost decided to kill off the unsalable mustang stallions and foals. Knowing that the rancher had even considered such a shameful act had killed the last of Pete's respect for his boss.

These were his thoughts as he rode one of Sun Dancer's mares, a stylish grulla that had the size, speed and intelligence to become a top cow horse. Pete planned on trying to convince Tyson not to sell this one to the Army at Fort Churchill.

He finished working the mare at a quick rein and began to twirl his lariat. Mustangs generally had a great fear of ropes; it came from the fact that they rightly associated a rope with pain. The grulla was no exception. Pete knew, however, that it was just a matter of time before the mare would think no more about ropes than flies buzzing overhead.

It was almost noon when he started back to the ranch headquarters. The day was bright and warm. Gauzy clouds stretched west clear over the blue-green Sierras and Pete could see dark thunderheads shadowing them. Most of the summer storms came in from the Pacific Ocean but few made it over the mountains. The Sierras seemed to catch the storm clouds and rip their underbellies so that the western slopes shone green, while out here on the eastern slopes it was dry and parched, except for a few isolated rivers and springs. Pete had been over on the California side of the mountains and all those trees had made him feel closed in. To a man used to vistas hundreds of miles in any direction, being hemmed in by forest and mountain was a disquieting thing.

He was thinking about dinner and trying to ignore the grumbling of his stomach when he saw a plume of dust coming his way from the ranch. Pete stood up in his stirrups and pulled his hat down low. He squinted and slowly it dawned on him that the approaching rider was . . . Candy on Sun Dancer!

He cussed out loud and touched spurs to the grulla mare, which was always ready to fly. Damn that girl. The palomino wasn't ready for her to ride yet! And no animal should be raced across this rough sage and rock-strewn country. Pete chose the best angle he could and made a line that would intercept them. He had his rope in his hand and if the gelding was a runaway, he hoped to have at least one shot at it before it passed.

As the angle narrowed, he had the distinct impression that Candy was not afraid and that she was actually racing the horse for fun. When she saw him, she threw one slender arm up and waved, then began sawing on the reins, trying to make the mustang turn in his direction.

"Candy!" he shouted. "Stop him! There's a ravine between us!"

She appeared to hear but not to distinguish his words as she smiled and kept coming. Pete yelled until his throat hurt. The ravine was choked with brush and totally invisible to an approaching rider from the opposite side, especially to someone foolish enough to be racing through nearly waist-high sagebrush.

There was nothing Pete could do. The palomino was just too fast and would reach the ravine first. When it did, there were only two disastrous possibilities: Either Sun Dancer would attempt to clear the wash and fail, or it would try to stop at the very last instant and its momentum and weight would propel them into the ravine.

Now Pete saw Candy's terrified expression. She had finally seen the yawning ravine. Candy screamed and pulled back hard on the reins but it was too late. Sun Dancer took the bit between its teeth, gathered itself and jumped.

The powerful animal seemed to rocket off the opposite bank, then hang against the sky for a brief moment before it arced downward, front hooves clawing as if that might gain it a little more distance. Miraculously, Sun Dancer's forelegs did clear the ravine and its rear hooves punched into the soft earthen sides, then churned for purchase. Pete watched the horse fight up and out of danger.

But Candy had lost her stirrups and seat. Terrified at going over backward and being crushed by the falling horse, perhaps she had tried to throw herself from the saddle and gotten hung up. Pete saw her fall across the palomino's right shoulder and that's when Sun Dancer twisted its powerful neck around and sank its teeth into Candy's leg.

She cried out in pain and then, to Pete's horror, the mustang tore her off its scarred shoulder, reared up and then stomped her into the earth. Candy's scream cut the air like a knife as the palomino whirled and raced for freedom.

"Candy!" Pete shouted as he hit the ground running.

He expected to find her dead. But when he rolled her over, he saw that she was still breathing. Her face, however, was covered with blood. Pete tore off his shirt and ripped it into bandaging strips, then managed to get the bleeding stopped as Candy began to moan softly. The entire side of her face was torn by those rock-sharpened hooves.

Her eyes opened and she stared up at him but did not seem to be able to focus. "Candy, I'm going for help!"

"No," she cried hysterically, "don't leave me for him."

It took Pete a moment to understand that she meant Sun Dancer.

"He won't come back for you. When you grabbed at his shoulder, he thought you were a cougar. He wouldn't hurt you again."

"Please don't leave me, Pete!"

He fought down a rising panic. The ranch headquarters was at least ten miles away across hard country and Pete knew he could not reach it in less than two hours on foot; the grulla mustang mare was nowhere in sight and had probably followed Sun Dancer back to their home ground.

Pete cradled her in his arms and began to talk to Candy in the same soft, reassuring voice Jack Kendall used in gentling mustangs. It worked. In less than five minutes, Candy was no longer hysterical but had become calm and was breathing normally. Pete was glad that she could not see the extent of the damage the palomino's hooves had done to her face. Still, there was only one real bad cut; the rest was just swelling and maybe a good surgeon could fix her up fine again. The main thing was that Candy was lucky just to be alive; if Sun Dancer's hooves and weight had landed directly on her head, her skull would have been crushed like an empty eggshell.

"We've got to get you to a doctor as soon as possible. We can't wait until tonight when they realize we're missing and then send people out to find us. I saw a cavalry unit camped about four miles to the east this morning. They had wagons and maybe a doctor. It's worth the risk."

She nodded. One eye was swelling completely shut but the other was open. "Can you carry me that far?"

"Nothing could stop me," he vowed as he slipped his arms under her back and lifted. She cried out softly and he wondered if the palomino had damaged her inside. If so, she could be bleeding to death internally.

Pete squared his shoulders and started walking through the sage. His eyes were fixed on a distant hill beyond which he hoped lay the Army camp. This was a gamble; if the patrol had departed, he would have wasted a hell of a lot of time and strength and never forgive himself. But if Candy was bleeding inside, then the gamble might save her life.

Pete doggedly marched on. Within an hour, he was staggering under Candy's weight. She weighed perhaps 120 pounds. If he had been able to shift her from one shoulder to the other, it would not have been so hard. But her dead weight soon became torturous. Pete tried unsuccessfully to ignore the twitching nerve in his neck that sent fiery impulses down his back and arms. His long horseman's legs were hard but their muscles were not accustomed to this kind of labor and soon began to knot and burn. Pete's shoulders ached and his arms radiated pain to his very fingertips.

Time and the miles passed with agonizing slowness. The sun leeched at his strength and once he blindly staggered forward, ignoring the ominous warning of a diamondback rattlesnake. The creature sank its fangs into his bootheel and Pete escaped unharmed.

Candy said little. Once every five or ten minutes, her good eye would flutter open and she would study the deep strain lining his face. But she was in such pain that he did not think she even recognized him. By the time he finally topped a rise and stared down at the Army encampment, Pete was so exhausted it took him several seconds to realize the gamble had paid off.

"Help!" he croaked in a dry whisper. "Help!"

They didn't hear him and he kept staggering on, thinking

angrily that if he were an enemy, they'd probably have seen him a lot sooner. When he finally was spotted, the camp reacted quickly and he was met by a squad of running soldiers. A sergeant took Candy into his own arms and with a shake of his head muttered, "Another half hour and we'd have been gone."

"Do you have a surgeon!"

"Yeah. This your wife?"

Pete shook his head with exhaustion. "Not yet, anyway."

"Bet she was pretty," the man said hopelessly.

"Not just pretty. Candy was beautiful." Pete scrubbed tears from his eyes. He guessed Tyson had been right when Jack had gotten his leg busted—they should have shot Sun Dancer.

Two hours later, the Army surgeon stepped out of his tent. He was young for a doctor, of average stature with strong features and an air of confidence that generated trust. Pete waited for the verdict.

"She's going to be all right," the surgeon pronounced. "Some broken ribs, probably bruised lungs, but no internal bleeding that I can detect."

Pete's numb legs almost buckled with relief as the doctor reached out and supported him, adding, "But we're both very concerned about her facial lacerations."

"Candy is awake?"

"Yes. The first thing she wanted to know was if her face was all right. I had to inform her that she has a very deep laceration across her left cheekbone—to the bone."

"How bad will it scar?"

"I can't say. Back at Fort Churchill, I have the surgical instruments necessary to do the finest surgery in Nevada. I come from a line of Boston surgeons and I assure you my credentials are of the highest order."

Pete wiped a hand across his eyes. "All right, so what do you want to do?"

"To minimize tissue loss and scarring, I must operate at once. Unless, that is, you or whoever is responsible would prefer a civilian surgeon."

Pete's temper flashed. "Hell no! Her father would want her operated on as fast as possible. So what are we standing around talking for!"

"Because the lady is a civilian and I'm an officer of the United States Army. I am sure I can get permission from my commanding officer. However, I need civilian authority."

"I'm giving that to you, damn it! Now, haven't we jawed about this long enough?"

The surgeon glanced at his commanding field officer. "Captain Henning, I ask you the same question."

Pete spun to face the captain and he was prepared to shake the hell out of him if necessary.

"Yes," the officer said decisively. "Bring her out of your tent and we'll load her in a wagon and leave at once." He twisted around to his sergeant. "Break camp!"

"Yes, sir!"

Five minutes later, Pete and the surgeon were crouched beside Candy in the wagon. Her face was swathed in bandages.

Pete studied the Army surgeon, remembering stories about the barbaric techniques sometimes used on soldiers at frontier outposts. "You sure you're good? If you mess up her face, Mr. Tyson will tear you apart—if I don't do it first."

He nodded without looking up from his patient. He had wavy brown hair and a square, aristocratic jaw. "When my tour of duty is completed next year, I'll return to Boston, where I'll practice on rich old women to make them look young again. But none will ever compare to this girl."

Pete nodded. "I'm glad you can tell she was pretty."

"Not was," the surgeon corrected. "Is."

For the first time in many hours, Pete relaxed.

CHAPTER EIGHT

Pete had been on longer wagon rides, but he couldn't remember when. They finally arrived at Fort Churchill just after midnight, but no one was sleepy. The surgeon's name was Dr. Madison and now he wasted no time in getting Candy into his neat military hospital.

"Pete, you can watch or go outside and wait. I don't care as long as you stay out of my way."

"I'll stay."

The surgeon wetted a sponge and carefully squeezed it almost dry and then spoke very softly to Candy. "This will make you drowsy and you'll fall asleep. When you awaken, I'll be here and you will feel much better. Do you understand?"

"Yes." Her voice was a whisper. She tried to smile and show him her faith in his ability, but the effort brought tears.

"Just relax, Miss Tyson," he said, placing the damp sponge over her nostrils. "Now, breathe deep and think of something beautiful. Trees and sunshine, the surface of a rolling river, flower petals floating on a pond."

Candy stared up at the surgeon until her eyelids began to droop and then closed.

"Let's get started," Dr. Madison said to his assistant as he removed the chloroform-soaked sponge.

The young enlisted man nodded and quickly began to help the surgeon. First they removed the temporary bandages, then they painstakingly cleaned all the dirt and bits of imbedded sand from the wounds. This took a long time and Pete noticed how the surgeon kept lifting one of Candy's eyelids to study her pupils. Every twenty or thirty minutes, he replaced the chloroform-soaked sponge over her nostrils and then checked her pulse.

When they were satisfied that the lacerations were absolutely clean, Dr. Madison wasted no time in selecting a tiny, hooked needle and thread. He used a pair of forceps to make perfect little stitches. The room was cool, but even so, the surgeon was soon perspiring heavily and so was Pete. Dr. Madison was very deliberate and unhurried, yet Pete understood that he was working just as fast as possible. He explained that there was a danger that Candy might become oversedated and have breathing difficulty, or go to the opposite extremity and awaken, thrashing in pain.

Pete marveled at the surgeon's dexterity. He glanced down at his own thick, work-roughened hands and knew that he could never do this kind of delicate work. Dr. Madison's fingers were long and very slender; this man had obviously never worked with horses or tools, but his skill was a beautiful thing to witness.

Pete lost track of time and count of the number of stitches. When the operation was finally over, Dr. Madison was so drained he had to support himself for a moment against the operating table. That made Pete understand the amount of concentration surgery required.

The assistant was allowed to do the final bandaging and he was skillful. Pete went outside and drank in the cool, fresh air. The night air braced Pete and cleared his mind. Fort Churchill was asleep except for a couple of sentries patrolling the grounds. This fort had been much busier before the war, but now was half empty because most of its soldiers had been sent back East to fight. There were only a couple dozen regulars and officers left. The rest of the occupants were civilian volunteers who were paid to keep the Indians and the miners from making war on each other. Fort Churchill served as an important recruiting station for the Comstock in addition to being a procurement facility for the kind of horses supplied by Tyson and a few other mustanging outfits. Tyson was the main supplier in this part of Nevada and, until recently, that was entirely due to the skill of Jack Kendall. Now, Pete thought, it's up to me until Tyson starts ordering mustangs shot.

"Miss Tyson is awake and wants to see you," Dr. Madison said, coming out to join him.

"How did it go in there?"

"Very well. She's young and I think her scarring will be minimal, something you may not even notice except in very bright sunlight."

Pete slumped with relief.

"You obviously care a great deal for Miss Tyson. Are you engaged?"

"Why do you ask?"

"Just curious." The doctor smiled. He reached inside his coat pocket and found a thin and very expensive-looking cigar. "Let's just say that I'm going to enjoy her convalescence. So will every other man on the post. I'm afraid that sick call will become a parade starting tomorrow."

Pete was not pleased with the observation. "Just don't keep her here any longer than necessary, Doc," he said, heading inside.

Candy's face was swathed in bandages but her voice was firm. "Pete, I want you and the boys to catch that horse and shoot him before he kills the next person who tries to ride him."

Pete tried to explain. "When you fell on his shoulder . . ."

She gripped his wrist hard. "Don't you see that it doesn't matter why he did it! The horse can't be trusted. Two people have already been badly injured. The horse must be destroyed!"

Pete nodded. He would not argue with this girl, not after what she had just gone through.

"Please go tell Father where I am before he goes crazy with worry."

"I'm on my way."

"Pete?"

He stopped and turned back to her bedside. "Yeah?"

"I'm sorry about Sun Dancer. I was wrong to want him but it's too late now. He's gelded. If you turned him loose, he'd never be able to reclaim a band and some stud would eventually kill him."

"I know that." He clenched his fists because it had all been such a waste. "So he can't be wild again and he can't be trusted under a saddle. He would never submit to a wagon. That leaves him with nothing but a bullet, doesn't it."

"I'm sorry."

Pete nodded and headed for the stables where he could borrow a good, fast horse.

It was breaking day when he found Tyson and every hand he could muster out on the range searching for Candy. When the man heard the story and Candy's instructions that Sun Dancer be shot, he was practically insane with anger.

"All of you," he roared, "stay out here until you find that animal. I want him brought back alive."

"Why?" Pete demanded to know. "Why not just let us shoot him out here on the range where he belongs?"

"Because I'm going to beat him to death with a single-tree, that's why! You're my head mustanger and that means you're responsible for doing as I've ordered!"

Pete nodded before Tyson struck out across the sage-covered land toward Fort Churchill. Tyson was riding a fine buckskin and would probably break its wind in his anger and stupidity.

"Well," a cowboy said, "where should we start looking, Pete?"

Pete thumbed his hat back. None of this set well with him, but at the same time, he could see that it made sense. Why take the chance that Sun Dancer would cripple or kill someone else?

"Half of you ride south toward those mountains and sweep the base, then turn east toward the salt flats and look for tracks." He twisted around and stood tall in his stirrups. "The rest of you ride toward those low hills. Fan out and make sure he isn't hiding in the arroyos."

"Where you going?"

"I'll ride toward the north, then angle toward the Carson River. More than likely, the stud isn't but a few miles from where he spilled Candy. He's trailing a pair of reins and is probably hung up in some brush."

Pete spurred his Army horse into a run. With any luck at all, he would find Sun Dancer by himself and bring him back to headquarters.

There was just one problem—there was no way in this world he could allow Tyson to beat Sun Dancer to death.

As the day wore on, Pete followed his instincts and tried to reason like a mustang. The palomino would circle back to home range and then search for any of his band that might have escaped capture. He would find them, but they'd already belong to another stallion. What happened then was conjecture; the palomino would surely challenge another stud for his mares and that challenge might or might not be answered.

There was a definite pecking order among wild stallions, even those fortunate and strong enough to possess mares. Pete knew that the palomino was the most feared of all the stallions on this range and had been for the past several years. Now that he was gelded, however, that might suddenly change. And if there was a fight, Sun Dancer would be seriously handicapped. There was a bit in his mouth and that would greatly diminish his ability to bite leg and neck tendons. Also, the saddle would prove cumbersome, though it would offer some protection.

Pete rode hard and by late afternoon he was galloping along a dry wash when he heard the sounds of two wild horses engaged in a terrible contest. Pete spurred his horse out of the wash and across the sage hills. The squeals, the snapping of teeth and the sickening thumps of hide being stuck by hoof were all familiar. Some men believed that stallions fought but did not kill their beaten opponents. They were wrong.

Pete and Jack had both seen beaten stallions left to die with their throats ripped or their legs and tendons badly crushed or severed.

He flew over a low rise and pulled his mount to a sliding halt. Down in a broad valley, he saw a band of mares scattered around the combatants. One was Sun Dancer, the other was a huge pinto stallion and they were struggling for their lives. The two animals were fighting with forefeet and teeth; their long, powerful necks were darting in and out like the head of a cobra, each seeking a vital point.

The pinto kept diving to its front knees trying to bite the palomino's foreleg. Sun Dancer was fighting the attacks off and it was obvious that the bit in its mouth was proving to be an insurmountable handicap. The pinto drove for the rear hocks and when it missed, its teeth snapped and they made the sound of a pitched horseshoe striking an iron stake.

Sun Dancer spun and delivered a crushing kick to the pinto's ribs that knocked the animal sideways. The pinto staggered and Sun Dancer reared, then came down on it with the same jagged hooves that had almost killed Candy Tyson.

Pete drew his rifle and fired in one smooth motion. His bullet whip-cracked across the sage and Sun Dancer whirled to run. Pete spurred forward. The pinto stallion was hurt, but even so it showed surprising speed as it gathered its band of mares and drove them away.

The chase was short and swift. Sun Dancer was lengthening its lead with every stride until, for the first time, it stomped on its trailing reins. Its head snapped down to the earth and it did a complete somersault in the air. It landed so hard it was stunned and by the time it was able to revive, Pete had it roped.

Sun Dancer knew the way of ropes. It had fought them and been choked into submission. Now, it stood trembling in wait.

"Easy," Pete said as he began to talk to the battered and bloodied palomino. "What do you want to fight that pinto for? Won't do you any good anymore."

The nervous horse danced and shook its head.

Pete waited until the palomino settled down and then he just turned his own mount around and lined out in the direction of Cross T. Sun Dancer came along behind as gentle as a pony.

"Pete Sills, you're a Judas, that's what you are. And before Tyson returns drunk enough to kill that horse, you had better decide how you are going to stop him."

Jack Kendall was waiting for him in the fading light. Jack, leaning against the bunkhouse without his crutches but with most all of his weight on his good leg, had his war bag packed and his bedroll tied up neat and tight along beside his Colorado saddle.

Pete reined in Jack's direction. Cowboys and mustangers alike pushed back their chairs and filed out of the cook-shack, but none of them said a word as Pete led Sun Dancer forward.

He stopped before the old broncbuster. "I guess you heard what Tyson is going to do to this horse."

"Yeah. Would you let him?"

"No," Pete heard himself answer.

Jack nodded to the palomino. "Musta been a hell of a stud fight, huh, old boy?"

He touched Sun Dancer on the shoulder. The animal snapped at him but Jack must have been expecting it because he pulled his hand back in time. Looking up at Pete, he said, "I never broke a horse after it has been landed on by a mountain lion. Won't be easy."

"You're taking him." It wasn't a question. Pete knew how the broncbuster's mind worked.

"Sure am." Jack slowly reached for the latigo and began to uncinch Candy's saddle. He lowered it and her saddle blankets to the dirt.

"Tyson won't like this."

"Don't matter to me," Jack said, taking his own blankets and setting them proper before he reached for his saddle. The effort brought a grunt from his lips because he had to lift and throw his saddle on one leg, but he did it.

"He may charge you with being a horse thief," Pete said. "That's a hanging offense."

"I know. Still don't change anything." He tightened the

cinch. "You did a fine job with this horse up to now, Pete. A fine job. I thank you."

Pete nodded in silence.

"If Tyson asks you, tell him I rode off to California."

Pete found that very amusing. "Hell, you don't even like California, Jack!"

"I know. Tell him anyways." Jack tied his bedroll and war bag to the saddle, then his rope.

He was wearing a six-gun and now he shoved his Winchester into the saddle scabbard under the stirrup.

"You got anything to eat?"

"Yep. Peewee filled my saddlebags."

"Jack. Will I see you again?"

Jack was still for a minute before he turned to face Pete. "I sure as hell hope so," he managed to say. "But I don't rightly know. You marry Maria before you quit this ranch, hear me?"

"You always did talk too damn much," Pete said, trying to smile and doing a poor job of it as he dismounted to shake hands. There wasn't a damn thing more either of them could think of left to say.

It was hard watching Jack try to get up into his saddle. Pete wanted to give him a helping hand, but he didn't dare. Jack had to try twice, but somehow he got his hurt leg over the high cantle and buried in his off-stirrup. They studied each other for a long time before Jack gave him the only thing that he had left to give.

"You're the best now," he said. "You remember that come hell or high water."

"I will."

Jack turned Sun Dancer around and rode off then as the mustangers came out to call their good-byes.

"Where's he going?" one asked.

"California," Pete replied absently.

"But he's heading east!"

Now Pete smiled. "Yeah. Must be lost already."

The man stared at Pete in disbelief for a moment, and then his surprise dissolved. He nodded with sudden understanding. "Reckon he is at that. Old Jack musta stayed here a mite too long."

When Tyson came back to learn that Jack had ridden off on Sun Dancer, he was so mad he almost fired them all.

"Where'd the son of a bitch go!" he thundered.

"California," Pete said.

"The hell he did!" Tyson swung on his other men. "Which one of you is going to tell me the truth!"

Not one man spoke, even though they had all seen Jack ride that palomino east. Pete felt a swell of pride to count himself among such men and he wished Jack could have seen how they all protected him.

Their silence seemed to unnerve Tyson. His lips grew white and his cheeks blew in and out. He balled his fists and turned to stomp toward the ranch house. Halfway across the yard, however, he stopped and whirled back to face them. "You son of a bitches had better not lie to me again. I pay your wages and I expect some loyalty."

"What are you going to do about Jack?" Pete called out. "Are you going to sign a warrant for his arrest? If you are, I'm quitting."

The heat washed out of Hugh Tyson. "No," he finally managed to say, "but I wash my hands of him. If he wants that palomino that bad, he can have him and good riddance to them both. They'll probably kill each other anyway."

That was all Pete wanted to hear. He turned back to the men and said, "I guess we had better get to work, boys."

During the next couple of months, Pete worked the mustang bands down south between Aurora, on the California-Nevada border, and Walker Lake. It was good mustanging country and one not often visited by professional mustangers. They were averaging fifty mustangs a week and that was as good as the outfit had ever done under Jack Kendall.

Pete worked himself and his riders hard. He alternated his time between catching wild horses and breaking the very toughest of the mares. There was not enough daylight to find time to eat, and he lost weight. Every few weeks they would trail the mustangs back to the Cross T Ranch and Tyson would quickly sell them.

Candy was home now, and when the bandages were removed, Pete could see that Dr. Madison had done a beautiful job. A month after the stitches were removed, even the faint red scar lines vanished. By October, when the cottonwoods were dropping their leaves and the nights getting cold, Candy appeared as pretty as ever.

Dr. Madison became a regular visitor long after his services were required. He came every Sunday for dinner and when Pete was at the headquarters, he could hear them laughing together inside. And though he thought he could tell that some of the hands felt sorry for him, Pete found he did not care a great deal if Candy still loved him or not. He was in charge of mustanging, and that was a heady responsibility and one that he meant to handle the best way he knew how.

That Thanksgiving, Pete and his weary mustangers were caught in an early snowstorm and had a bad time driving forty-three head into the ranch corrals. They arrived to see Candy and the surgeon leaving in a shiny sleigh bedecked with bells and ribbons.

"I'm afraid you lost the boss's daughter," one of the mustangers told him sadly. "I was sorta hopin' you'd marry that girl and take over this outfit one day."

Pete shook his head and smiled. "Sorry to disappoint you, but I'm happy doing what I'm doing right now without all the headaches involved in running this ranch."

"Tyson don't run anything. He stays drunk most of the time."

"Why don't we just work a little bit more and talk a little less? Go get some feed for these mares. Ask a couple of the men to help you."

The mustanger nodded. "I didn't mean no offense, Pete."

"I know that, but a man's mouth has a way of getting him into trouble more often than not. Let's just do our jobs."

When the mustanger left, Pete turned to look out at the snow-covered hills and he still could see the Army surgeon and Candy sleighing across the land and hear the jingle of bells. It seemed to him right then that she was heading out of his life for good. So be it. Candy wanted an educated man, someone who could spout poetry and whose hands were soft and clean. Pete doubted he could ever be that man. He was homespun and rough-cut. He was a mustanger and a broncbuster and would be until he could no longer sit a wild horse.

"Hey, Pete!"

He turned around to see Tyson marching toward him. The man was swaying just enough to show that he had been drinking heavily. Pete waited beside the corral. He didn't trust his boss when he was drunk; Tyson could get nasty and combative.

The rancher placed his hands on the rails. "You see Candy and that Army officer?"

"Sure."

"What do you think about it?"

"What do you mean?"

"About them, god damn it!"

"They looked like they were enjoying the sleigh ride," Pete said.

Tyson eyed him with unconcealed disgust. "Hell, man, I used to think that you and my daughter might get married."

"Not likely." Pete looked him in the eye. "Besides, I thought you wanted Candy to marry an educated man. Someone just like Dr. Madison."

"He wants to go back to Boston and that would be the last I'd see of her.

Now Pete understood.

"Those are good horses you brought in today, but I'll tell you something," Tyson breathed. "The future is in cattle, not mustangs."

"Mustangs like these have done well for us."

"Yeah, but they're part of the old way. Pete, I know you don't want to hear this, but I intend to bring another five thousand head onto the Cross T range this spring."

"The range won't take that many."

Tyson lit a cigar. "It will," he said very deliberately, "if we get rid of the mustangs. Catch those we can sell, eliminate the rest."

Pete tried to keep the heat out of his voice. "Do you mean shoot the stallions and the foals? Is that what you're getting at?"

"Now simmer down, damn it! I didn't say that." Tyson stared into the distance. "Look, my daughter is riding out of here on Thanksgiving Day and I'm alone. Candy says she told me there was a dance and dinner at Fort Churchill, but I forgot."

He puffed on his cigar. "The thing of it is, I'm going to lose that girl if you don't start spending more time here at the ranch. You got to do something besides chase horses."

"That's my job."

"Maybe I want you to change your job around. You need to start learning about cattle and finances. Read and broaden yourself."

"What about the mustangs? I'll quit if you shoot even one."

"Don't say that," Tyson warned. "Not until you know the dollars and cents of ranching more than you do right now."

"My mind won't change," Pete said stubbornly.

"It will the day you become my son-in-law and a part owner of the Cross T." Tyson grinned. "How does ten percent of my profits sound? If you marry Candy and do things the way I want, you can have a piece of this ranch."

As good as it sounded, Pete knew he wouldn't sell his soul for Candy or the Cross T. Besides, he'd seen the happiness in Candy's face when she had ridden out in that sleigh with Dr. Madison. They had been all bundled up under blankets and anyone could tell they were in love.

Tyson's flask was in his hand. "Listen," he said, "why don't you join me tonight for dinner? Maria has cooked a turkey with all the trimmings."

Before Pete could answer, the man threw an arm across his shoulders and was pulling him toward the house. Pete knew he was in for a long afternoon, but he had not seen Maria for weeks and maybe that would make the day bearable.

As soon as he confessed to Tyson that it was over between him and Candy, this sudden interest in his future would be forgotten. Tyson might even fire him in his anger.

Pete smiled. He figured his days on Cross T were numbered, but that didn't mean he was fool enough to pass up Maria's turkey dinner.

Thanksgiving Dinner had been wonderful, but Christmas was one of the worst Pete could ever remember. Maria's mother, old and always frail, had suffered a serious stroke and, as the new year began, she lay partially paralyzed. Pete rarely saw Maria during that winter. When he did, there was such a sadness in her that they talked only about the sickness and what the doctor from Yerington said. The old woman was ready to die. Hour after hour, she prayed the rosary beads and it was the general feeling among everyone that she was simply used up by years of hard work. Watching Maria, Pete vowed that she would not suffer such a difficult life. He would find a way to offer her much more.

In January, they found a stallion and eight yearling foals shot to death over near Rockland. The animals were terribly thin, for it had been a tough winter; most of the mustangers believed that they were shot out of mercy.

Pete was not so sure. And while the mustangs were far below their normal weight, they were strong and would have been able to last through the final months of winter. He could not help but wonder if Tyson had anything to do with this, but he did not ask.

Maria's mother died in February and the funeral was held on a bleak, sunless afternoon. Mrs. Kelly could not have weighed eighty pounds and was buried not far from Mrs. Tyson. A hard wind was blowing off the Sierras and anyone could see that more snow was coming. When Pete looked at Maria, she seemed to have aged five years. He could not help but wonder why the two of them had not gone away and sought something better, and then he realized they had stayed because Maria was in love with him.

Pete stepped over to Maria's side and then he put his arm around her shoulder. The gesture was not lost on anyone present. Tyson looked furious and some of the cowboys and mustangers were clearly surprised. As for Candy, she smiled and took Dr. Madison's hand.

It seemed to Pete right then that the die was cast and that this spring would mark an end and a new beginning to his life. He thought he knew how, but he was not sure.

And for some reason, he thought of old Jack Kendall and just knew that he would see his friend again. Jack had always said that endings and beginnings ought to come as often as the seasons to keep a man from getting jaded.

Perhaps that was true. All that Pete knew for sure was that, with Mrs. Kelly's passing, everything was changing.

CHAPTER NINE

The last winter storm of the year struck the high desert range a week after the funeral and it snowed heavily for three days. The weather stayed cold for another week so that the snow formed a thick icy crust that horses dropped through, injuring their fetlocks. Travel was almost impossible.

Pete and the mustangers used the time to mend their gear and rest their weary bodies. They fixed broken straps and made new lariats. They oiled their boots, bridles and saddles until the leather no longer squeaked.

When the weather suddenly grew warm, the snow vanished within a single day and the mustangers eagerly returned to the range. They found dead Cross T cattle, but less than fifty. It was the bullet-riddled mustangs that chilled Pete's blood.

He might not have discovered them had it not been for the circling buzzards. They had been driven up into a maze of rugged canyons and then slaughtered. There were twenty-six: two stallions and the rest colts, fillies and a couple of mares too old for saddle or harness.

The grisly sight was one that Pete would never forget and it sent him racing back to the Cross T Ranch headquarters. He wanted some straight answers from Tyson. This was Cross T range and whoever had slaughtered those mustangs had done so with Tyson's approval. All that remained was to hear the rancher admit he'd ordered the kill.

Candy opened the door and when she saw his face, she knew that something was wrong. In as few words as possible, he explained to her what he had found and ended by saying, "Your father must have ordered those mustangs shot."

She had paled. "Come inside."

"Where is he?"

"He had to go away on business, Pete. I didn't think he'd really do it." Her voice was filled with despair. "I thought I'd talked him out of it but he has a new herd of cattle arriving soon and the range is in bad shape. If there's not enough feed, he could lose everything this summer."

Pete didn't give a damn about the new herd of cattle; the range was already overstocked. "That doesn't make what I saw right!"

"I told Father that. But what I say has no effect on the Cross T anymore. You see, I told him that Dr. Madison and I were engaged to be married this summer. James's Army enlistment will be up in the fall, and we'll go to live in Boston."

"Congratulations," he said solemnly. "I'm sure you'll be very happy."

Candy managed to smile. "And I hope that you and Maria will get married too. You need a woman who likes the heat and dust. One who is willing to scrimp and tough things out while you mustang."

Candy walked over to her father's bar and poured them both whiskies. "I never was," she said, handing him a glass. "I'm sick of these blazing hot summers and freezing winters. Of dirt, biting horseflies and ticks. I want to go where there is excitement, where people dress beautifully, dance, go to operas and plays and talk of things besides cattle, horses and the damned weather."

There was an undercurrent of vehemence in her voice

that surprised him more than her admission. "I always thought you loved this ranch."

"I hate it! This ranch killed my mother. She died as much of loneliness as anything. She used to tell me stories about Washington. As a child, she lived in a big house on the Potomac River. Her family used to go on moonlit boat rides. People lit bonfires along the water and she said they talked and sang and it was enchanting."

Pete saw a faraway look creep into her blue eyes. She had already left Nevada. "James comes from a wealthy family. One that lives with refinement and elegance."

She shook her head a little sadly. "I guess that makes me look very shallow, but I can't help it. My mother felt the same way, but she never told anyone except me. I think, had it not been for Jack Kendall, she would have left this country and perhaps still be alive. She was every inch a lady, you know. Educated in a very fine Philadelphia girls' school. You should have heard the wonderful stories she told me of her childhood and early years!"

Pete felt a sudden rush of pity for this girl. Candy had always been strongly influenced by the memory of her mother, but Pete had never quite realized how very greatly until now. "Being a ranchgirl, I'll bet you'll make quite a sensation among the high society."

Candy laughed. "That's exactly what James says. He has promised me my very own horse but I must ride it sidesaddle. Can you imagine!"

Pete could not. Anyone who had ever seen this headstrong rancher's daughter flying across the prairie on the back of a half-wild mustang would know she could never completely fit into a staid Eastern riding club. A club where the ladies probably wore fine leather gloves and rode fat, sleek and blooded horses that had never sent their hooves smashing into a prairie dog or badger hole.

"You'll have to be very careful not to let them know how good with horses you really are."

"I've been playing roles all of my life. I'm a very good actress, Peter."

She lifted on her toes and kissed his cheek. "I don't think we'll ever have the chance to talk like this again. So I'll say good-bye now. Take Maria away from this place and never look back."

"It might save my life if you told me who your father hired."

Candy turned away from him but Pete caught her by the wrist and pulled her close. "I'll find out anyway. I can't run away and let your father hire men to slaughter mustangs."

"I don't want you killed!"

"My best chance of staying alive is in knowing what and who I'm up against. Now who shot those wild horses?"

She looked right into his eyes for a moment before she whispered, "Lester Barron. Father hired him as cattle boss again. Until the new herd arrives, he's supposed to kill the mustangs he can't capture for selling at Fort Churchill."

"Thanks," Pete said quietly. "At least now I know what I'm up against. But I can't understand why he'd rehire a man like that."

"My father is confused and bitter. Since losing Mother and now me, he has changed into someone I hardly know anymore."

"I have to oppose him, Candy."

He touched her lips with his forefinger. She was about to say he'd be shot if he interfered. But what Candy didn't understand was that a man could never run from his conscience. If he allowed Lester to sweep this range of mustangs, Pete knew he would always be haunted by the vision of dead mustangs waiting for the buzzards.

Had he chosen to describe in detail what he had seen

early this morning, Candy would understand. But that would cause her pain and she was leaving soon; he did not want to give her such a vision to carry east.

"I'm going to ask Maria to marry me. If she says yes, we'll leave right away."

"Of course she will."

Candy threw her arms around his neck and hugged him tightly. She began to cry and he heard her say, "I'm so very happy for us all, Peter. I really am."

They decided to be married in Carson City. On the day of their wedding, an exuberant bunch of mustangers and cowboys galloped up to the chapel. Intent on raising hell, they quickly changed their minds when they discovered that the priest was Michael O'Reilly, a hulking, stern-faced Irishman well known for bashing the heads of the unruly together. The ceremony was beautiful and included the priest's rough-voiced warning that Pete had better take good care of his lovely new wife.

Pete slipped a twenty-dollar gold wedding band on Maria's finger and they were pronounced man and wife. When he kissed Maria, the spectators finally began to hoot and clap their hands. The priest smiled broadly. He crushed Pete's knuckles in a powerful grip and then said he expected to have the honor of baptizing their first infant within a year.

The chapel had a small flagstone courtyard. It was surrounded by high adobe walls covered with vines and bright flowers. Because Maria was half Mexican and the daughter of a very saintly woman, the Mexican population showed up in full force for the wedding ceremony and reception. They brought their Spanish guitars and violins and many jars of their fiery aguardiente to share, a liquor that made the cowboys gasp and their eyes water. Aguardiente was said to be three times stronger than whiskey and when Pete obliged to drink a toast, he believed it.

Their wedding reception was the first real party after a cold winter and everyone was in a festive mood. Tables were laden with roasted chicken, mounds of beef, lamb and baked trout fresh from the snow-fed waters of the nearby Carson River.

When the music started, Maria told her new husband that he was expected to dance. Pete had never been much of a dancer, nor had he expected his new bride to be. Maria proved him wrong. She was graceful and feather-light in his arms. She was even able to make him look good without appearing to do so. Waltzing with Maria was something he wanted to do the rest of his life.

But then, almost as if a cloud had sealed out the warmth of the sun, smiles and laughter dissolved and the music died.

"What is wrong?" Maria asked with sudden alarm as they stood together on the dance floor.

"We have visitors," Pete said, angry at himself because he was unarmed, while Lester Barron and Tyson were obviously prepared for a gunfight. "Step away from me while we talk, Maria."

In response, she held his arm even tighter.

Tyson walked right up to them and Pete could smell the liquor on his breath. He was shaking with rage. "You both walked out on me without even saying thanks for all the years I supported you. I deserved better."

"So did the mustangs I found slaughtered."

"I need all the grass and water I can get."

"Those mustangs were on open range."

"My range!" Tyson struggled for control and he forced his eyes to Maria. "Congratulations, you're very beautiful today. Now you must convince your new husband to mustang somewhere else."

"I go where my husband goes. You do not rule open range."

Lester growled. "I told you it was a waste of time."

"Shut up!" Tyson snapped. "Listen, Pete. I won't try to stop you from catching mustangs on free range, but neither can you object to my killing them. It works both ways."

"Maybe the sheriff feels differently."

"He doesn't," Tyson said with a strict smile. "In fact, he understands that the ranchers keep this town alive. We have talked and he agrees there is nothing anyone can do to keep me from gunning down every last mustang I can't put a rope on and sell. Any way you look at this, you lose. No one would be foolish enough to help you and you can't mustang alone."

"I will help him!" Maria said.

"How noble. But how meaningless."

Pete said, "You might be surprised how many we can catch by ourselves before you shoot them."

Lester barked a laugh. "You'd both best be careful. A lot of stray lead will be flying around. Be a real shame to see a pretty woman get hurt by mistake."

Pete's fists knotted. "Get out of here before I throw you both out."

"Stay away from my land and out of my business," Tyson warned, jabbing a finger at Pete. "Or you'll be leaving a very beautiful widow to grieve."

Maria's eyes flashed and she said something in Spanish. Suddenly, the Mexicans began playing the fandango. The music was rich and strong; it spoke in a proud voice that mocked Tyson's deadly warning.

Maria lifted and shook the skirts of her wedding gown so that Pete could see her trim ankles. She pressed her fingertips together overhead and began to dance. In an instant, Tyson and Lester were forgotten as Maria whirled to the throbbing beat. Her thick, shiny black hair surged with her body and she was mesmerizing. There was a smile on her sensuous lips and her eyes locked with Pete's.

He completely forgot about Tyson and the danger that awaited them in the months to come. All he could see and think about now was Maria. His mouth felt dry with desire and when she threw her head back and laughed happily, he could not believe that he had actually won the love of such a beautiful and spirited woman.

They used what little money they had to buy supplies necessary to begin mustanging. It was spring, the weather was cool. Even though they had received a late snow, it had been a very dry winter and the ground had not saturated itself in preparation for the long, blistering summer ahead.

When Pete gazed up at the towering Sierras, only their highest peaks were mantled white and he knew that the spring runoff would be far below normal. The Carson River would almost run dry by late September and even the Walker would become little more than a creek.

Out on the high desert range, everything depended upon water. Right now, things looked fine but Pete knew that blistering winds would soon suck the moisture out of the earth, leaving the range powder-dry. He did not know how Tyson justified buying more longhorn cattle to add to his already overstocked range. The man was operating solely on greed and was a damned fool.

For three weeks, he and Maria mustanged down near Goodhope Springs. It was very difficult with only two riders and whenever a clever stallion began to peel away and take its mares, Pete had to ride like blazes and try to cut it off. He was successful only part of the time. But Maria loved the excitement of the chase and never grew despondent, not even when a day's hard riding left them with an empty horse corral. Pete found that the best way of catching the mares was to try and lasso the stallion and then tie it while they rounded up its confused harem.

There were a lot of times when Pete and Maria wanted to quit driving themselves so hard. But whenever they heard the distant sounds of rifle fire or saw buzzards gathering to fly in their ever-tightening rings, Pete knew that Tyson and his men hadn't quit.

By early June, he had busted and sold thirty-three mares and almost as many colts and fillies to a horse buyer who would peddle them cheap to small ranches and farms. Pete had to let most of the stallions be because they were practically uncatchable with only two riders. He did not mind this because a stallion without mares was almost impossible to shoot; they were too alert to allow a man like Lester or one of his cowboys to approach within rifle range. Given time, the strongest stallions would probably leave this range in search of new mares.

It was mid-June when a cowboy crossed their trail. He was a tall, horse-faced young man from down near a new boomtown named Candelaria and was on his way to Reno.

"I'm a hell of a fine bronc rider," he said, thumbing his hat back on his head and cocking his left knee around his saddle horn.

"I could use some help," Pete told him. "I've got about ten mustangs that need topping and I can't seem to find the time to catch them and bust 'em both."

"Sorry, but I mean to win some of that bucking contest prize money they're offering at the Reno fair this year.

Maria perked up. "What contest is this?" she asked quickly.

"Oh, I heard about it from a fella got off the stage the

other day. Besides the horse race and all the other stuff they usually have, the folks that run the fair wanted to have a bucking contest for the crowd."

He snapped his fingers. "Say! I'll bet you could take these broomtails of yours to Reno and get paid good money by letting the cowboys ride 'em!"

Pete said, "You think so? I never heard of such a thing."

"Well, they're doing it! Sending fliers out on every stage telling all about the contest. I used mine up to start last night's campfire, but I can tell you the first prize is a hundred dollars and there's fifty for the runner-up."

"Pete?"

"Sure," he said. "Why not? We could use a little extra money."

"Dang!" the rider said. "The last thing I meant to do was to drum up even more competition for myself. Way I hear it, cowboys and broncbusters from all over the state are coming to ride."

"When is it?"

"Two days from now," the cowboy said. "You and your wife need a hand driving those mustangs?"

Pete nodded. "Much obliged. We could for a fact. We'll feed you well for your trouble."

"Was hopin' you might," the cowboy said, unwinding his leg from around his saddle horn. "Let's get them started."

Reno, or Lake's Crossing as the old-timers still called it, was in the midst of a boom. The Central Pacific Railroad had announced that it was building its half of the transcontinental railroad through town, causing a flurry of land speculation. There were bridges built over the Truckee River, which flooded out the eastern part of town almost every spring, but the river was so low this year there was no danger. The streets were rutted sloughs of mud, but even so, the town had a permanent air about it that was unusual in boom-or-bust Nevada.

They drove the mustangs right through the center of town and caused quite a stir among some of the local merchants, who seemed a little testy, considering this was their biggest money-maker of the year. At the fairgrounds, they were greeted warmly and Pete was able to rent all of his mustangs out to the bucking contest for a dollar each. He used part of this money to pay the five-dollar entry fee.

"What are the rules?" he asked.

"Rules? Hell," the man said, "the only rules we have is just to ride the animal to a standstill and not get piled."

"What if he isn't much of a bucker?"

"Then you don't win. Look, there's a certain amount of luck to winning this. You draw a bad horse, one who don't buck, well, there isn't much you can do except spur and whip him real hard and try to create some excitement. That's what this fair is all about. Excitement draws the crowds."

Pete scrubbed his chin. The idea of trying to make a mustang buck harder was sure a new twist on things. "You got any other horses?"

"About twenty more. There will be a drawing at noon in front of the Red Dog Saloon on Virginia Street."

"He'll be there and so will I," a familiar voice said.

"Jack!" Pete grabbed his hand and pumped it hard. The man looked good. He hadn't changed a bit. "Damn, I should have known you'd be here for this!"

Jack grinned. "I wouldn't be if I'd have known I'd be riding against the likes of you, Pete. The truth is, I come mainly to race Sun Dancer."

"He's here?"

"Sure. I've won two or three match races on him over in

Elko and across the border in western Utah. Getting so nobody will bet against him anymore."

"Well, let's have a look at him."

"Soon as I pay my entrance fees," Jack said, plunking down ten dollars, five for the bucking contest and five more to enter the horse race.

"You marry Maria Kelly like I told you?" Jack asked over his shoulder.

"Sure did."

The old broncbuster smiled broadly. "Good for you, Pete! I knowed you was smart enough to see through Candy and pick the right filly."

I almost wasn't, Pete thought as he and Jack started across the crowded fairground to see the palomino. They passed all kinds of exhibits and even an organ-grinder with a chattering monkey that snatched pennies from delighted children. There were games and lots of food. Over near the barns was a new breed of cattle that came from England and was called Hereford. Pete just glanced at them. They were red and white, pretty but delicate things that would never stand up to hard range conditions found in America. They looked like little puppies compared to the majestic Texas longhorns.

Pete explained that Maria was resting in a hotel room which he had to pay someone five dollars to vacate. He also told his old friend about Candy's love affair with the Army surgeon and that they were getting married and leaving for Boston.

"They sound well-matched. How is Tyson handling it?"

"Kinda hard," Pete said. He did not intend to tell Jack about the personal threats or the slaughter of mustangs. If Jack got involved, there would be blood spilled for sure and the law was on Tyson's side. Prison would kill the broncbuster and he was too damned good to hang for killing the likes of Hugh Tyson.

"If I win anything in the bucking contest today, I'll use it to bet on Sun Dancer tomorrow," Jack said.

"You're that sure he can win?"

"Nope. But he's got a damn good chance of it. Pete, you ever think about owning a ranch?"

"Lots of times."

"Maybe you and Maria ought to come to Elko with me. I'm thinking of buying a little spread about ten miles out of town. Sits right up against the Ruby Mountains and it's the finest mustanging country you ever laid eyes on."

"Nothing I'd like better," Pete said. "But the timing is off. I need about six more months in this country."

"Why?"

"I just do," he replied quietly.

"Suit yourself," Jack said, not quite successful in hiding his disappointment. "The offer will always stand."

"I know that," Pete said. "And I think we'll take you up on it by fall."

"Working together like in the old days would be mighty fine," Jack said, happier now. "That Elko country is crawling with mustangs. This is about the time we ought to be getting the catch corrals built, Pete. Not later."

"Yeah," he hedged and then gave out a low whistle when he saw the big palomino again. "Sun Dancer, I forgot how good and strong-looking you are!"

Jack hooked his thumbs into his belt and let Pete make a fuss over the mustang gelding. "Finest horse I ever owned," he said proudly.

"Did you ever break him of the mountain lion fear?"

"Nope. I just make it a point not to lay on his shoulders and everything is fine between us."

Pete shook his head. "Now why didn't I think of that?"

They had drawn their horses and Pete was pleased to learn he had gotten a rangy but thin bay mare that looked like she could buck off chiggers. The competion was keen, but Pete hadn't seen anyone make a ride that he wouldn't have made look even better.

"This is a damn shame," Jack said, his face hard and uncompromising. "Look at that son of a bitch spur and quirt that buckskin! Look at that!"

Pete was looking. The buckskin wanted no part of bucking. It just crow-hopped around a little and gave up. The man on its back was furious and kept punishing it.

Finally, Jack could stand no more. He strode out into the arena and yelled loud enough for everyone present to hear, "You keep that up, I'll rip you the hell offa that animal and use my spurs on you!"

"I paid five bucks to show my stuff."

"You showed it plain, mister. And I don't like what I've seen so far, so get offa that horse. Drag your butt outa this place before I kick it up between your shoulder blades!"

The cowboy swore, but he jumped off the cowering buckskin and stalked away in a fury.

Three more riders had a try and two of them were thrown for a loop. The one that rode was all over his saddle and hanging onto the horse's mane.

"It's your turn, Jack. Good luck!"

The broncbuster yanked his battered Stetson down hard. Those in the crowd that recognized him told everyone else how good he was and Pete could almost feel the tension building as Jack came to stand beside the strawberry roan that the cowboys had eared down and held waiting in the arena.

Jack swung his saddle up onto the animal's back and when it exploded, he simmered it down and then tightened his cinch. He was thicker in the middle and ten to twenty years older than the other competitors, but he swung aboard that mustang like it was the most natural motion in the world for a man to do.

"Let him go," he ordered.

The cowboys pulled a bandanna from across the roan's eyes and released the agonizing grip on its twisted ear. The roan shook its head for a moment and then it launched itself into the sky and landed stiff-legged. The spectators yelled with approval and when the roan exploded up again and then twisted, Jack spurred it hard. The animal grunted and came down twisting. Jack quirted it once, then once more across the rump. The quirt made a whipping sound and lifted dust from the animal's coat. Pete knew that it stung like the very devil but did nothing more.

The roan grunted with pain and reared up on its back legs. Some of the women in the crowd grabbed their children and the men all made an "ohhhhing" sound. Jack drove the horse into a leap with his spurs.

The roan landed on all fours and then gave up. It cringed and, at Jack's urging, sort of bounced around and around the arena until it smoothed out into a nice, even trot. Jack pulled up on the reins and the animal stood trembling.

Pete saw Jack's lips moving and though he could not hear the words, he knew that they were soothing but nonsensical, nothing more than a litany of reassurance.

The crowd had fallen silent. Jack seemed to have forgotten them anyhow as he plow-reined the roan one way and then the other.

The man in charge of the bucking contest was not impressed. "Next rider!" he shouted. "Pete Sills, get in here and give these folks the kind of a show they came to see!"

Pete grabbed his saddle and headed out to see if he could win some prize money on the bay mare.

By the time he had the saddle on and was ready to ride, the bay was soaking wet with fear. It was tall but very thin and cow-hocked in the back legs. Pete looked over to see Jack standing beside Maria. They were both watching him intently. He swung up into the saddle and said, "Let go of her ear and stand back."

The mare was frozen. Pete slammed his spurs into her sides and she grunted with pain and bucked without any heart. He quirted her a few times but she didn't get mad or try to get even. She lowered her head and Pete gave her all the rope she wanted, but the mare didn't use it to her advantage but instead seemed to want to hide from all the shouting spectators.

"Damn it anyway!" Pete cussed. "Of all the danged horses, I had to choose one like you!"

He could hear the man in charge yelling at him to use the mare with his spurs and quirt. The hell with him! This mare wanted nothing more than to please.

Pete pressured her with his knees and the mare took a few tentative steps forward. "Come on, girl," he said, plow-reining her just like Jack had done a few minutes before. "Show your stuff and maybe someone will buy you for a kid's horse."

The mare's head lifted and she trotted almost stylishly around and around. Pete stopped her by the fence and dismounted to face Maria and Jack.

"Hell of a fine ride for a real broncbuster," Jack said, his eyes shining with pride and approval.

"Maybe so," Pete drawled, "but kind words and two rides like we just made won't even buy us a plate of beans and a glass of river water."

"To hell with it," Jack said, taking the saddle off for him. He watched the next contestant begin to punish his bronc, to the delight of the Reno crowd. "Let's get out of here.

We'll just have to get our money back tomorrow when Sun Dancer wins the big race."

Pete nodded happily. "I guess we weren't meant to win bucking contests like that."

"I'd be mighty disappointed in us if we did," Jack said as they picked up their Colorado saddles and headed across the fairgrounds.

They had dinner together and though it wasn't fancy, it wasn't beans either. Mostly, they talked about mustanging. Pete got some ideas on how to catch them with just two people. He listened while Jack told him about a man from San Francisco who brought over a narcotic and tried to drug mustangs at the water holes. Problem was, he over-dosed a few good saddle horses and was damn near strung up on a telegraph pole before being run out of town.

"Tell us about this spread you have your eye on in the Ruby Mountains," Pete said.

It was a subject that Jack was eager to talk about. "Well, sir, it isn't much to look at," he began, "but with a little elbow grease and a few dollars, we could add a new roof and a wood floor. The land is what's best about it. Almost a thousand acres of pine and meadows. Prettiest country you ever did see and covered with mustangs. When the trans-continental railroad comes through Elko, it will be perfect for shipping horses east or west."

"What about water?"

"Sweet as honey and plenty enough for a couple of mus-tangers—but not a big cattle rancher."

"Sounds perfect," Maria said.

"Sure does," Pete agreed. "How much they asking for it?"

"Five hundred cash. They're practically giving it away. I've already saved two hundred and if we bet on Sun

Dancer and he wins, we'll have the rest. Right after the race, we can leave and . . ."

"No," Pete said too quickly.

Maria covered his hand with her own. "We'll come soon, Jack."

"You got trouble here? What's to stop you from coming now?"

There was nothing in the world that Pete would have liked better than to tell Jack that he needed his help, but instead he mumbled, "Just some loose ends is all."

Jack spread his thick-fingered hands up in a gesture of resignation. "Suit yourselves."

He stood up and winked at them. "Best be going to sleep down at the livery with my horse. It's going to be a lucky day for us tomorrow."

"I hope so. But most of the other horses will have little riders weighing half what you do, Jack. They'll either be riding bareback or with those funny English saddles that don't weigh anything."

"I know that. I've looked at all the entries and there are a few blooded racing horses entered. But I'm still telling you to bet every cent you can beg, borrow or steal on Sun Dancer. I know horses and this one will make believers out of people who say mustangs are long on endurance but short on speed."

Later that night, Pete held Maria and gazed into her eyes. "If we can get long odds, I think we ought to take Jack's advice and bet everything on Sun Dancer tomorrow."

She was silent for a long time. "But what if we lose? What will happen to all the mustangs down south that we might have saved if we didn't bet? We have to have supplies."

"I know. But we also need enough money to build corrals

and maybe even hire someone to help us," Pete said. "It's a risk I think we ought to take. How about it?"

Maria kissed him and held him very tightly and that was all the answer he needed.

CHAPTER TEN

The course of the race was a city block at the eastern edge of town. All the cross streets had been roped off and the racehorses would have to go around twice before crossing the finish line. The fact that the horses would have to slow in order to round each of the corners was to Sun Dancer's advantage. The tall thoroughbred racehorses weren't very agile and they needed to build up a long head of steam.

The race wasn't until noon, but by eleven both the inside and outside perimeters of the track were lined with spectators. Up on the rooftops, grown-ups as well as children perched expectantly. Pickpockets cruised through the crowd and there were hawkers selling everything from popcorn to shots of whiskey.

The racehorses were being kept in a big rope corral and though there were guards to keep out the crush of inquisitive bettors, the situation was hopelessly chaotic. The horses were nervous, they could sense the excitement and one, a dapple, kicked anyone who came too close. Men were shouting out bets, seeking better odds, fighting to speak to the riders and owners in order to glean as much last-minute information as possible.

Pete and Maria arrived late and before they could push through the throng to reach Jack and Sun Dancer, they ran into Dr. Madison and Candy. The newlyweds were studying a flashy sorrel racing mare that had captured everyone's fancy.

"She's pretty," Pete said, coming up behind the couple. "But you had better place your bets on Sun Dancer to win."

Candy spun around with surprise. "Peter, Maria! How nice to see you here!"

She did look happy to see them and so did the doctor.

"We thought you'd be living in Boston by now," Pete said.

"We're leaving tomorrow," the surgeon said, "but we're not looking forward to the long stagecoach ride."

"Peter, did you say that Sun Dancer is actually racing today?"

"Yes. He's over there in the middle of that crowd somewhere." Pete watched her face as she turned and scanned the crowded field, searching for the palomino. He could not help but remember how much Candy had wanted to ride Sun Dancer in this race. "Would you like to join us in finding them?"

"Of course. Who's riding him?"

"Jack. Who else?"

"But he's much too big!" Candy protested. "He'll outweigh any other rider by at least fifty or sixty pounds. How long is the race?"

"A mile," Pete said. "Two times around this block. The finish line is over there by all those flags."

The doctor pulled out a gold pocket watch. "It's nearly eleven-thirty. If we are going to find them, we'd better get started."

It did not take them long to locate Jack and Sun Dancer. When they drew near, they overheard the old broncbuster explaining to a crowd of skeptical listeners that his horse was a mustang and the scars across his shoulders were caused by a mountain lion. The bettors weren't favorably impressed. Sun Dancer was a working horse and had never been blanketed or kept in a clean stall, which meant his coat was rough and unkept-looking. His legs were perfectly straight, but too heavily muscled. Pete now saw that, compared to the blooded racing horses he would be up against, Sun Dancer appeared coarse. It was also true that the palomino was deceptively calm. While most of the racehorses around him were prancing and putting on a spirited show for the critical bettors, the golden-colored mustang looked sleepy.

"I wouldn't give you fifty to one on that animal," a man said as he shook his head and hurried away. "Not up against the sorrel and that other horse from Kentucky."

"You're probably right," Jack said, managing to look almost ashamed of his horse. "But miracles can happen."

"Are you gonna ride him with that big old cowboy's saddle?"

"Yeah."

"Christ, man. Haven't you seen what the others are using? They all have little men and those English saddles that don't weigh more than ten pounds. That saddle you have must weigh sixty."

"At least," Jack sighed with agreement.

"Mister, no offense, but it'd take a miracle for that horse of yours to win."

"I suppose."

Pete almost laughed outright; obviously, Jack wanted everyone to think that his horse was slow. He held his laughter and waited until the bettors passed on, shaking their heads.

"Nice work," Pete said to the mustanger. "Keep talking like that and the odds *will* be fifty to one."

Jack turned. For an instant, his surprise at seeing Candy showed, but whatever his thoughts were, he hid them well. "Candy, it's nice to see you looking so fine. And you," he added, stretching out his hand to the surgeon, "you must be the Army doctor that Pete and Maria told me about."

When they shook hands, Dr. Madison winced. "I've heard a lot about you too, Jack. And this horse." He studied the animal closely. "There was a time when I would have shot this animal on sight."

Jack studied him closely. "We all make mistakes and that would have been a big one. Nothing wrong with this horse."

"I'm glad that you took him away from the Cross T," Candy said, breaking the tension. "It wasn't the horse's fault. I can say that now. I even wish . . ."

"What?" Jack asked.

"That I could turn back the clock and do some things differently. I still wish I could have ridden that horse in this race. It was something I dreamed about for years."

"Darling," the surgeon said, "that's ridiculous."

"Why?" Candy turned on him suddenly.

Dr. Madison was caught off guard by the directness of her question. "Well," he stammered, "for one thing, it's dangerous. And for another, it's not the thing for a lady to do."

Candy's cheeks flushed. "My dear man," she said imperiously, "I am afraid that you are just going to have to accept the fact that I'm not one of your Eastern hothouse flowers. And as long as we are in the West, I'll act as I please!"

"But this horse almost killed you!"

"I don't care about that anymore. If it hadn't been for the accident, we'd never have met. And right now, what bothers me is that Jack and that saddle are too heavy. I don't believe it's fair to Sun Dancer to be at such a disadvantage. If I ride him . . ."

"Absolutely not! I forbid you to do such a thing!"

Pete suppressed a grin. If there was one thing he had learned over the years from watching Candy, it was that you never told her she could not do something. It only made her all the more determined to prove you wrong.

She was absolutely furious. "Jack," she said, choosing to ignore her husband, "I know how you feel about me, but I want to ride this horse. He needs someone light to win, and I need to do this for myself. May I please ride Sun Dancer?"

"Your husband's right. There'll be a lot of money bet on this race and it'll get rough out there. You could get hurt."

"Legally, I could make a case that this horse was stolen from my father," Candy said.

Jack's face hardened. It had been the wrong thing to say and Candy realized her mistake at once. "But I won't do that, even if you refuse to let me race him today. Please, Jack. I was a fool to race Sun Dancer through rough country. If he were an ordinary animal, he'd have crashed into that dry wash and I'd have been crushed to death or crippled for life. I owe this animal something. Can you understand what I'm trying to say?"

He studied her for almost a full minute. "Okay," he said quietly. "For your mother's sake."

"Thank you," Candy said, turning to look up at her husband's face. "I need you to understand, too."

"I still think you're insane."

Candy smiled tolerantly. "It will give me another story to tell my new Boston friends when I have them over for tea. Think how notorious it will all sound!"

"You aren't even dressed properly. And I absolutely forbid you to ride in your petticoats."

Candy stomped her foot down hard. "Damn it, there you go with that word 'forbid' again! You'll have to learn that I don't accept that from anyone." She shrugged. "But I'm afraid you do have a good point about this skirt. There's not enough time to return to our hotel and change into a riding outfit."

"You can use mine," Maria said. "We can find a place close by and change."

Candy smiled. "Thank you! Then it's settled. Shorten the stirrups. Maria and I will be right back. She reached into her purse and removed a wad of greenbacks. Darling, bet it all on me and Sun Dancer to win."

As they hurried off, Jack read the doctor's confused and exasperated expression and said, "She ain't ever going to be completely tamed, Doc. About the best you can do is to keep her snubbed as close as you can to the bedpost."

"I know," Dr. Madison said with a shake of his head as he counted the money. "This is our honeymoon and I've tried but that doesn't work either."

While they were gone, Pete made their bets. Among the three of them, they bet almost a hundred dollars at twenty-to-one odds that Sun Dancer would win. The sleek sorrel thoroughbred was an odds-on favorite, with a dapple gray racehorse a close second.

Jack finished shortening his stirrups just as a man with a megaphone began to shout for the entrants to bring their horses to the starting line. Now Sun Dancer seemed to wake up. His head lifted proudly and he pranced toward the starting post. Men who had not seen fit to give him any hope of winning did not change their minds, but they no longer dismissed his chances entirely.

"Mount your horses!" the announcer shouted. "Mount your horses and bring them to the starting line!"

"Where the hell are they!" Dr. Madison cried frantically.

"I don't know," Jack said as he led the palomino forward, "but if they don't get here when the gun goes off, I'm going to have to ride with my boots hanging a foot below my stirrups."

Pete saw them. They were caught in the crowd, waving, calling for help.

"Let's go!" he yelled as he and the doctor began to force their way to the women.

"Racers, at the starting line!"

"No!" Jack thundered. "Give us just another minute."

A horse squealed and someone was kicked. The racers were all mounted, their horses dancing and spinning. Handlers were trying to keep order and a man bellowed in pain as he was trampled by a rearing horse.

Pete broke through to the women and then he grabbed them and they fought their way back toward the line. The gun went off and a hoarse shout erupted from the crowd.

Jack grabbed Candy and threw her into the saddle as the other horses lunged away in a thunder of flying hooves and dirt. Candy jammed her feet into the stirrups and grabbed the saddle horn as Sun Dancer exploded across the starting line. He was a good twenty yards behind but when they rounded the first corner and disappeared, he was moving like a flash, ears down, head low to the street, tail streaming out behind him.

People were shouting and the police were trying to clear the starting place because the horses were coming across that line and needed room to run.

Pete grabbed Maria and followed Jack as they hopped up onto an already crowded buckboard. Someone yelled for them to stay off but one look at Jack's face was enough to silence the protest. It seemed like an eternity before Pete heard a shout.

"Here they come!" the announcer bellowed. "Ladies and gentlemen, give them room!"

Now the crowd parted as the ground shook. The lead horse was the sorrel thoroughbred and it was followed by a bay, then the gray. The animals were running hard. Nostrils distended, hooves snapping out and clawing up big hunks of dirt. The riders were all little men, professionals who sat low to their horses' necks and used a whip as though it were an extension of their arm.

"Where is . . ."

"There!" Jack shouted. "She's in fourth place and coming on fast."

Indeed, as the leaders swept by and then slowed to take the corner of the next block, Pete could see Candy and Sun Dancer and they were flying! The crowd screamed with delight as the big palomino streaked past, devouring the distance that separated himself and the blooded racehorses.

Maria was jumping up and down, yelling for Sun Dancer, as the last five horses shot past. She grabbed Pete by the shirt. "Can he do it?"

"Sure he can!"

The crowd quieted. They could hear the screaming voices of others on the opposite side of the block as the race swept past them.

The officials hurriedly stretched a red ribbon across the finish line. The official with the megaphone was yelling, over and over, "Ladies and gentlemen, once again, stand back! And give these horses and their brave riders a big . . ."

A collective roar drowned out the announcer as Sun Dancer and the sorrel thoroughbred barreled around the final corner. They were charging toward the finish line. It was a magnificent sight! Both animals were running flat out and hardly seemed to touch the earth as they ran neck and neck, stride for stride, toward the fluttering ribbon.

"Who's winning!" Dr. Madison shouted.

There was no way to tell because the horses were coming almost straight at them. Pete watched Candy and he had the vision of a very pale but excited young lady hanging onto that saddle horn for dear life. She was bent forward and urging the palomino forward with every fiber of her being.

The crowd's roar funneled down the canyon of humanity, rising in intensity as they neared the finish line. It was a crescendo that lifted the animals high on its crest. Hundreds of screaming, nameless faces. Forelegs and hooves reaching, manes and muscles stretched and lungs working like tortured bellows. Sun Dancer floating thirty feet at a stride as he burst through the red ribbon and the crowd screaming as if it had suddenly gone insane. Maria throwing her arms around everyone and kissing them as Pete tried to wipe happy tears from her cheeks.

Dr. Madison leapt from the buckboard and followed Jack into the crowd toward the victorious horse and rider. Pete held Maria tight and howled with joy. "We won six hundred dollars!"

They celebrated that night with steak and champagne. Pete and Maria gave Jack three hundred dollars and told him to buy that horse ranch in the Ruby Mountains. They would become partners.

Candy was still excited about the horse race. She kept telling them about it and even revealed how one rider had tried to knock her off but that Sun Dancer had bit his hand as they swept past.

It was after ten o'clock when Jack stood up and said, "I want to get an early start for Elko, so I'll say goodnight."

Candy threw her arms around his neck. Not once had the subject of the Cross T and her father been broached, but now she said, "I'm glad you're leaving this part of the country for good. I just wish I could talk Pete and Maria into doing the same."

"We will. Soon, I promise," Pete said as he shook Jack's hand. The very last thing on earth he wanted was for Jack to know about the mustangs that were being slaughtered.

"I'll buy that ranch for us," Jack said. "I'll expect you and Maria before the first snowfall."

"And I'll expect you to have that new roof on," Maria said with a laugh. "And a wood floor, too!"

"It's a promise."

Jack left them, looking mighty pleased with life. As he made his way through the crowded dining room, people saw the smile on his weathered old face and they grinned, too.

"You really ought to be going with him," Candy said quietly.

"We've been through all this before," Pete said.

"I know. But you didn't listen. Lester hates you, Peter. He wants you to return and when there are no witnesses, he'll try to ambush you."

"I'm not looking for trouble and we'll stay away from it whenever we can. But Maria and I are bound and determined to capture as many mustangs from that country as possible before we leave."

"That's what I was afraid you'd say." Candy raised her glass of champagne with a tight smile. "Then I offer you and Maria a toast—to health, happiness and, most of all, to a long life of mustanging together near Elko."

They touched glasses and drank. But the celebration was over and Candy's warning hung between them and dampened everyone's spirits. Pete and Maria soon said good-bye to the newlyweds and left them alone.

The fun and laughter was over. It was time to go mustanging.

"Stay low," Pete whispered as he and Maria crawled to the top of a ridge. Pete removed his Stetson and inched his head up to peer down at the wide, arid valley beyond and the stallions preparing to fight.

"Ease your head up slowly," he told Maria. "Not many

have seen what you are about to witness. It'll be unforgettable."

"Will they kill each other?" she asked.

"I don't know. Fighting is nature's way of making sure that only the strongest reproduce."

To Pete, it was obvious that the dun was the older and more experienced fighter. He was covered with scars and one ear was missing. The animal was powerfully built and knotty with muscles.

The black was young and flashy. He had a blaze face and three white stockings. He was the taller of the pair and his excellent conformation led Pete to believe he might even be one of Sun Dancer's proud offspring. But the black had only two fillies that most likely had been driven away by their sires when they reached breeding age. This was another of nature's ways to prevent inbreeding and weakening of the species.

Both stallions had driven their bands a safe distance away and now the mares and the fillies stood at opposite ends of the battlefield watching.

"Here goes!" whispered Pete, unable to keep the excitement out of his voice.

At that instant, the stallions drove forward at each other. Ears pinned back, yellow teeth bared, they dropped to their knees, heads and teeth darting for the fragile legs of their opponents. Suddenly, they were up and the dun wheeled and kicked the black. The blow was loud a quarter of a mile away and Pete winced to think of its force.

The black staggered, parried the dun and tried to grab it by the neck. The dun's superior weight slammed the younger horse over and it rolled, but before the dun could rear and stomp it, the black was scrambling to its feet. Its head streaked out and its teeth bit into the dun's shoulder. Blood poured and when the dun twisted away, the black's teeth snapped like the cold steel of a bear trap. The dun lashed out with its sharp front hooves and opened up a deep slash across the black's ribs.

Both horses squealed and began to kick at each other, each apparently hoping its rear hooves would strike a hock or break its opponent's leg bones.

The black was getting the better of the exchange. Here, weight was of little advantage, easily offset by the younger animal's quickness and superior endurance. The dun stumbled in the hindquarters but when the black spun around and lunged to finish it, the dun suddenly crumpled to its front knees. Its massive head shot out and its teeth locked on the black's exposed foreleg. The black had been tricked and now, caught by surprise, it was desperately trying to break away.

The black squealed, only this time it was a different sound, a hurt cry as it tried desperately to pull free. Pete shook his head, feeling drained by the spectacle. The fight had lasted under five minutes and yet the sheer fury of it made it seem like hours.

"It's decided," he said. "The dun will hang on until the leg is useless and then he will have won."

Maria watched the black stallion thrash helplessly. She saw the dun bury its rear hooves in the soft ground and let itself be dragged forward a little.

"Can't you stop it!" she cried. "He's such a beautiful animal."

"It's the way it must be," Pete said. "It's not our place to interfere."

Maria scooted back down the ridge and ran to their own horses. She yanked Pete's Winchester out of its scabbard, levered a shell into the chamber and began firing.

At the sound of the rifle shots, the dun released its bite

and sent its mares and those of the defeated black fleeing across the valley.

"Look!" Maria cried. "The black is limping but not too badly. His leg cannot be broken."

Pete nodded wearily. He stood and hurried down to vault into his saddle. He would rope the black stallion and geld it immediately. If it survived the leg injury, it would make a damn fine saddle horse and command top dollar at Fort Churchill.

But Maria had other plans. "I want him!" she shouted. "If we are going to catch mustangs, I need a fast horse."

Pete nodded reluctantly as he charged down the slope, shaking out his loop. Saving the black's life had given Maria the right to claim this horse for her own. The black was a lot finer animal than the one he rode. Pete was about half angry that he hadn't thought to drive the dun away first.

Jack Kendall had taught Pete that if a mustanger learned where wild horses drank, he could catch them. Mustangs could go two days in hot weather without water, three if the days were cool.

They had followed the dun's trail and learned that he used three water holes roughly twenty miles apart. These water holes formed a triangle and, at two of them, Pete had tied brightly colored pieces of cloth called "spooks." The spooks were hung from brush and trees and kept the wary dun and his mares away from those water holes. The third water hole was left undisturbed and now, as Pete and Maria waited in hiding, they knew that the dun and his band of mares would be very thirsty after traveling a sixty-mile circuit without a drink.

It was late afternoon. The day had been hot and it was just starting to cool when they heard the band approaching.

"Just wait until they've had their fill and are too water-logged to run," Pete whispered.

Maria nodded. She had a rope in her hand and had been practicing but it was obvious that she was unsure of herself.

They heard the first of the horses splash into the watering hole and listened to their eager sucking noises as they drank. Pete counted off the minutes. Having been spooked at his other two watering holes, the dun would be especially nervous; the slightest sound or scent of a rider would send him flying into his mares and driving them to safety. Pete carried five ropes across his shoulders and saddle horn and Maria had two more. Seven chances altogether to run down and lasso the waterlogged mustangs.

They heard the dun begin to stomp the water impatiently. That was the signal Pete had been waiting for. He nodded to Maria and they lifted their ropes and then cracked them down hard across their horses' rumps. They came flying out of the wash side by side. The dun and his mares scattered, their hooves clawing at the muddy banks. A pretty chestnut lost her footing and tumbled before scrambling to her feet. Pete swung his loop three times and caught the chestnut. He spurred forward and then flipped the slack from his rope over the mare's rump and reined away at a sharp angle. The rope cut the hind legs of the mare out from under her and she went down again. Before she could recover, Pete was tying her legs and leaping back into the saddle to rope another mare.

The mustangs were bloated with water. The gallons that sloshed in their distended bellies hurt them with every stride and they were easy to overtake and rope. Every time, Pete would lasso their necks but then flip his slack around behind their rear legs and bust them to the ground. It was hard, rough and very effective. Pete heard Maria yell with triumph and he twisted in the saddle to see her tying a mare that lay stunned. Pete laughed and waved, then vaulted back into his saddle and struck out after yet another of the mares.

Pete caught three more before the dun and the rest of its mares vanished over a ridge and escaped into heavy brush. After a distance of nearly seven miles, Pete and his lathered mount were ready to quit. He tied the last of the mares so that her head was roped and bent to her tail. This was a method that Jack had taught him and one that Pete found particularly effective; it did not hurt a mustang, but ensured that they could not escape.

When he returned to the water hole, he found Maria proudly waiting for him with two mustangs she had captured.

He yelled, "Nice work! You have a real talent for this—you're a natural-born mustanging woman!"

She laughed. "It is easy to work hard and well when you are helping the man you love. But what do we do with them now?"

Pete thought that over very carefully. He could try to break the mares out in the open but that was always dangerous. A wild horse has a tendency to run if not confined and no one had to tell Pete that riding a bucking mustang through brush and rock was very dangerous. Inside a corral, however, horses were forced to buck in circles and the man in the saddle did not have to concern himself with the horse stepping into a badger hole. It left his mind freer to concentrate on the ride.

"That pole corral we built last spring," he said. "It's not more than fifteen or sixteen miles away. It has good water and grass, so I reckon we'll fix it up and break them right there."

"I would like to try that, too," Maria said.

"Broncbustin'?"

"Yes."

Pete shook his head and grinned. "Sorry, pardner, but I can't afford to lose a good hand, especially when she is the only one I have. And for . . ."

His eyes caught a glint of sun on metal and his words fell forgotten from his lips.

Maria tracked his eyes to a point in the distance and she saw them too. "Lester and the Cross T men?"

"I'm sure of it."

"Mr. Tyson said that he would leave us alone, Peter," she reminded him.

Pete forced a smile. "Sure he did. And why shouldn't he? After all, we're helping him rid the range of mustangs. Every horse we catch gives him a few more blades of grass for his damned cattle."

"Promise me we'll stay far away from them. I do not trust Lester Barron. He would use any excuse to kill you."

"This is open range," Pete said. "And I mean to stay out of their way as long as they stay out of mine."

They heard the faraway sound of scattered rifle fire. It made faint popping sounds and the riders they watched disappeared.

Pete ground his teeth together in helpless anger. He would bet anything in the world that they would see the buzzards circling tomorrow morning.

CHAPTER ELEVEN

Pete and Maria continued to mustang, using the method of "spooking" the water holes. They kept finding dead horses and several times it was all Maria could do to keep Pete from riding toward the distant sounds of rifle fire. The mustangs were becoming fewer on this range; those that escaped capture or slaughter were the fleetest and most intelligent.

What they were seeing more and more of were Cross T cattle. It was painfully obvious that Tyson and Lester were flooding the rangeland with Texas longhorns. By midsummer, the temperatures soared to over a hundred degrees. Mud around the water holes began to crack and the bawling noises of hungry cattle filled the hot, still valleys.

In late July, a Cross T mustanger named Jenkins rode out to their camp and his news was gloomy. "Tyson wants every mustang cleaned off this range by the first of September. You can see his cattle are getting weaker."

"Then why doesn't he sell them?" Pete asked.

Jenkins was a thin, worried-looking man who now squatted on his lean hams and drew the makings for a smoke out of his vest pocket. He deftly rolled his cigarette and flared a match off his bootheel. When he answered Pete's question, twin streams of smoke jetted from his nostrils. "Prices are way off. Every rancher west of the Rockies is having a hell of a tough time this year."

"So Tyson has got himself in a crack and can't find a way out."

"Yep. 'Cept in a whiskey bottle." Jenkins scowled. "You ask me, he's like a cornered cat and he'll claw anything that tries to touch him."

Pete frowned. "This will never be good cattle country. Mustangs and sheep can do pretty good, but not a bunch of cows."

"I know. Everybody tried to warn him, but Tyson isn't a man who takes good advice kindly."

That was the understatement of the day. "So what happens next?"

"I don't rightly know except that it won't be good," the mustanger said in a gravelly voice. "Tyson is drinkin' damned hard and I think the man is goin' crazy. Maria, when you and Miss Candy were there, the boss seemed to keep a rein on hisself. Now he spends most of his time drinking alone. Lester Barron is pretty much calling the tune at the Cross T. I put up with it as long as I could stand. I know you can't think much of me anymore, Pete. Don't blame you, either. I've shot maybe fifty head myself this year."

Pete looked away. He would never be able to understand how a mustanger could kill wild horses.

"Why?" he asked softly.

Jenkins squinted hard and studied his cigarette a long time before answering. "I needed the job. I'm thirty-four years old and figured I'd found a good home at the Cross T. With cattle prices shot to hell and ranchers failing everywhere, there are a lot of good cowboys out of work right now. When me and some of the boys quit a couple of days ago, all Lester had to do was to go into Yerington and he had as many hands as he needed. He hired a bunch of hard cases."

Pete looked up quickly. "Gunmen?"

"That's what I hear."

Pete avoided Maria's eyes but he knew she would be more worried than ever now. "Do you want to work for us, Jenkins? We can't afford to pay you wages, but you could take a piece of the profits from the mustangs we sell."

Jenkins inhaled deeply, spit a shred of loose tobacco. His skin had a gray pallor and he looked a lot older than thirty-four. The man was a good mustanger, but not the kind who could make it on his own.

"I think you're playin' a real dangerous game, Pete. I ain't got the kind of guts you do."

"Tyson said he'd leave us alone as long as we stayed out of his way. We've had no trouble so far."

"If he doesn't want to help us," Maria argued, "then don't try to talk him into it."

"You're right."

Jenkins shook his head. "It ain't that I don't want to help you, Pete. It's just that you haven't seen the kind of men that are drawing Cross T wages these days. All the old crew is gone. Scattered from Oregon to Texas. But we had some good times while it lasted. I was always proud to ride with you and old Jack Kendall. We was the best there ever was at mustanging."

"Nothing ever stays the same, does it," Pete said wearily.

"Nope." Jenkins sniffled and coughed. "I heard you saw Jack Kendall in Reno."

"That's right."

"Did you watch Sun Dancer and Candy win the big race?"

"Yeah. It was something to see."

Jenkins grinned. "Damn! I wish I could'a seen them. When Mr. Tyson heard about it, he almost went loco he was so damned mad. He was a-yellin' that the palomino still belonged to him and that he was going to swear out a warrant for Jack's arrest. Said he wanted Jack strung from the limb of a tall tree for horse thievery."

Maria was alarmed. "He couldn't do that, could he?"

The mustanger shrugged. "I dunno. A man can't just ride off with another man's horse—even if he did plan on killin' it. There are some who say Jack is mustanging up around Elko. That right, Pete?"

Pete squinted into the harsh sunlight. About five miles out on the salt flat, he could see a dust devil twisting into the cloudless sky. Toward Pine Grove the land lay flat with heat waves rippling like water. What if Jenkins was still on the Cross T payroll and had been sent to discover Jack's whereabouts?

"I couldn't say."

"You mean you won't say."

Pete met his eye. "Either way, it's the same answer. Why are you so interested?"

The mustanger fidgeted. "I sorta thought Jack might be needing some help. Best man I ever worked for. Besides, the way things are going around here, I figured it might be a good idea to find a change of scenery."

"Then Elko might be a good place to start," Pete said evenly. He was now convinced that Jenkins was being honest.

The man stuck out his callused hand with two fingers missing, both pinched off between his rope and saddle horn. "Thanks. I sure wish you and Maria would come along with me. There ain't nothing here but burnt grass and damn little water. Before it's all over, there's also going to be a lot of cattle bones bleaching in the sun."

"How many mustangs does Tyson think there are left?"

" 'Bout two hundred. Mostly, they're running in the Wassuk Range between us and Walker Lake. Up in those tough mountains where they're hard to catch. There is this one band, led by the handsomest chestnut stud you ever laid eyes on. Everyone wants him, but he's too smart to catch. Lester tried to shoot him a couple of times but he won't get caught within firing range. That's why he's ordered those fancy new rifles."

"What are you talking about?" Pete asked suddenly.

"The boss ordered some hunting rifles with telescopic sights. He'll use 'em to kill off the rest of the mustangs. Hell, Pete, he's even bragging about how he could make money by charging folks to go hunting that chestnut and the other bands of mustangs."

"The mustangs won't have a chance."

Jenkins nodded. "You got that part of it right," he said. "That chestnut will think he's safe and that's when either Lester or Tyson will put a bullet through his head."

Pete took a deep breath. "You want to draw me a map in the dirt and show me where you last saw him running his band?"

Jenkins hesitated. "I sure wish you'd think it over twice about buying into that kind of trouble."

"He's on open range, isn't he?" Maria asked defiantly.

"Yeah, but . . ."

"Then we have as much right to catch him as Tyson and Lester do to shoot him. Please draw my husband a map."

The mustanger ground his cigarette out in the dirt. He tore a branch off a piece of rabbit brush and then he smoothed a patch of the powdery earth with the sole of his boot. "All right, Pete, here is the East Fork of the Walker River and . . . oh hell."

"What's wrong?"

"Nothing, except I gotta live with myself. You want, I'll show you where he drinks and I'll even help you catch him."

Pete suppressed a smile. "You sure?"

"Yep. But we split it equal between the three of us, so I get a third of what we get from selling any horses we catch. Agreed?"

Pete looked at Maria, who nodded. "All right, it's a deal," Pete said. "Maria and I sure appreciate the help."

"There is just one other thing I forgot to ask for."

"I'm listening."

"If we catch the chestnut, you break him and sell him to me for fifty dollars."

"That must be one fine animal."

"He is," Jenkins said. "Best-looking thing I've seen since Sun Dancer. Maybe next year, he could race and win in Reno."

"Maybe so."

They tied their horses and walked to the crest of the ridge and dropped down to study the hills beyond. They were like the waves of an ocean stretching as far as the eye could see. Blue-green pinion and juniper pine. At first glance, Pete could see nothing, but then he noticed how the green in one fold of the earth was a slightly different color and when he squinted his eyes, he saw that it was grass and knew they had found the chestnut stallion's watering place.

"Is this where you saw him?"

"Yeah. We were over on that far ridge. Musta been about a month ago. That stud has about fifty mares. You got any ideas of how we're going to catch him?"

"We'd never get close enough to rope him in this country without killing ourselves."

"The stud knows that." Jenkins shook his head. "Me and the boys couldn't figure out a thing. These hills just get rougher and steeper to the east."

"Can you show me the trail he used to come to water?"

"Yeah."

"Did he lead, or does he get some wise old mare to do that for him."

"He led."

"Good." Pete sleeved sweat from his brow. "What time of day did he come?"

"Midmorning." Jenkins motioned off to the west. "Lester crawled through the brush to that point up there by those rocks. About the time he was ready to fire, the stud saw him and whirled. His shot went wide and they all got away."

Pete glanced up at the sun. They only had about two hours until darkness and they would need every minute of it.

As Pete expected, the trail used by the mustangs was narrow and it twisted through the sage. The earth was beaten down by their hooves so that it formed a gulley. Using a foot trap properly was something very few mustangers had mastered and a trick that Jack Kendall had believed extremely valuable. Basically, it involved digging a shallow hole squarely in the center of the trail and burying a noose. Another hole was then dug perhaps ten feet away and there a mustanger hid, concealed under brush until the arrival of his quarry. When the stallion stepped through a screen of twigs and dirt, the sound of cracking branches told the mustanger exactly when to pull the noose tight. At that moment, it was usually wise to have the rope tied to some immovable object and run like hell before the enraged stallion could stomp you to death.

The mustanger had to go to great lengths to conceal the fact that he had set his lure and was hiding close by. This meant that he needed to make very sure that there was not the slightest smell of man or sight of a foreign object anywhere. Even a broken branch on a piece of sagebrush would be enough to warn the stallion.

Jack had also taught Pete to drop fresh horse manure around the foot trap and his own hiding hole because it masked the human scent.

They had finished the trap around sunset. Pete and Maria had climbed inside and spent a long, difficult night waiting. Over and over, Pete had tried to think of anything that he had done wrong. Jenkins was a good man and would remove all signs of his retreat into the hills. They had swept the trail, used plenty of horse manure and set the noose down into the hole perfectly. The rope was completely hidden and Pete believed that everything had been done properly.

Morning came slowly. Maria had insisted on spending the night in the hole beside him but Pete doubted either of them would ever do it again. When the stallion finally did come, Pete was afraid his legs would be so cramped he'd be unable to move and that Maria would be equally helpless. They had decided that when the stallion was caught, the best thing to do would be to run, leaving the rope tied to a small juniper tree.

The hours dragged by slowly. Pete and Maria could see the growing sunlight filter through the brush they had piled over their heads. Jenkins was supposed to charge out of hiding and put a second rope over the chestnut's head. Between them, they could control the animal.

Pete looked at his wife, who was streaked with dirt and whose hair was covered with pieces of sagebrush from the covering they had placed overhead. "Well," he whispered, "how do you like mustanging from a hole in the ground?"

"With you, it is bearable. But my legs have fallen asleep."

"Mine too. Jack never told me about this part."

"You've never done this before?"

"Nope. And I never will again. Jack said it was a mighty

hard way to mustang. The only time he tried it was when his own horse broke a leg. Jack was fifty miles out in the middle of nowhere and not about to walk. He needed a mustang and this was the way he caught it."

"If we catch this stallion and perhaps even his mares, can we leave then?"

Before Pete could reply, he heard a mustang snort and his body tensed as his breath caught in his throat. They were coming.

He waited, trying to visualize the stallion as it moved cautiously down the often-traveled path to drink. Would it see something amiss? Suddenly, he heard branches crack and then the stallion trumpeted a warning as Pete yanked on his rope. Pete tried to leap upward, but his legs were dead and he only managed to throw his upper body over the lip of the hole. The chestnut saw him as his mares bolted into the sage, scattering like quail. The stallion was enraged. It hit the end of the rope. The juniper tree shivered as the chestnut began to fight the rope. Then it saw Pete and lunged at him. Pete threw himself back into the hole to shield Maria. The stallion reached down, sank his teeth into Pete's heavy jacket and plucked him from the earth as a hawk might a prairie dog. Pete shouted and the horse tossed him sprawling. Pete was wearing a six-gun but he didn't want to use it unless he had to.

Suddenly, Jenkins came flying out of the brush and when he threw his rope, his aim was true. He dallied around his saddle horn and pulled away hard. The stallion lunged after him but hit the end of Pete's rope. Caught between the tree and Jenkin's horse, it screamed in anger.

Pete grabbed Maria and pulled her out of the hole. "We've got him now! Steady!"

Jenkins knew what he was doing. Knew that all that was necessary was just to keep the stallion stretched between himself and that juniper tree until it settled. Pete would get mounted and set another rope over its head and the battle would be won.

"Wooweee!" the mustanger shouted. "I got me a racehorse!"

Pete spun to get his own horse, which was well hidden behind some distant rocks. He took six strides and then he heard the booming of high-powered rifles. A slug ripped into the heavy muscles of his upper leg, tearing away flesh. Pete yelled and tumbled as more shots bracketed the high ridges.

Maria screamed and then came running for him.

"Get down!" Pete yelled, reversing his direction and trying to crawl back to the hole. "Stay back!"

Jenkins caught a bullet in the chest that ripped him off the saddle and hurled him to the ground. His rope flew from his saddle horn and the stallion began to plunge wildly until two more bullets knocked it down to stay.

Pete screamed in anger and pain as Maria grabbed his arm. Bullets were pocking the dirt all around them as they threw themselves back into the hole.

"You're hit!" Maria cried.

"Not bad. Keep your head down!" he said between clenched teeth.

Maria tore her skirt and fashioned a bandage. She held it tightly against the deep wound but the bleeding did not seem to want to stop. Feeling faint, Pete helped her make a tourniquet and that staunched the flow of blood.

"We've got ourselves in one hell of a spot this time," he gasped, yanking his six-gun out of his holster. "Pinned down in the middle of nowhere."

"They'll have to come to us, won't they?"

"Yeah," he answered, looking up at the rim of their hole.

"That's the one thing we have in our favor. To kill us, a few of them are going to have to die, too."

"No one wants to die," she said. "Maybe they will go away."

Pete nodded. He could hear the chestnut stallion as its hooves clawed uselessly at the sage. He shifted his weight to one leg and removed his Stetson. In one swift motion, he raised himself and fired a single bullet into the stallion's head. The animal sighed and its body convulsed, then went limp.

Bullets swarmed overhead but Pete had already ducked for cover. His eyes glistened wetly. "You should have seen that animal," he choked. "No wonder Jenkins wanted him so bad. Neither of them had a chance."

Maria touched his lips. "I do not believe it is also our time to die," she whispered.

Pete gripped his gun tighter. "Neither do I!"

CHAPTER TWELVE

It was a standoff. Pete and Maria sat crouched in their hole as the day wore on and the sun beat at them with merciless intensity. Down in their hole, the temperature rose past one hundred degrees. They had a canteen, but it was only a quarter full. Pete grew feverish from his wound and loss of blood. He drifted in and out of consciousness as sweat poured from his body. Maria used her share of the water to dampen and cool his face.

"We've got to get out of here as soon as it's dark," Pete murmured. "No matter what, we have to get out!"

"We will," Maria said with more assurance than she could have felt. Her eyes glanced up to track the progress of the sun. "Another two hours. Go back to sleep."

He did and when he awoke, it was sunset. Pete studied his leg. Maria had removed the tourniquet a long time ago and replaced it with a tight bandage. The blood was caked blackly almost the entire length of his pants leg.

He shook his head, trying to clear the cobwebs from his fevered mind. "Maria, have you seen them moving yet?"

"No."

"But they will come," he told her. "They have to finish us off."

"Why not leave us to die slowly? Isn't that more their way?"

He had to concentrate hard before he was able to answer.

"Maybe so. We can't take that chance. We have to get to our horses."

He shifted his weight until he was kneeling on his uninjured leg. "As soon as it is dark, I may need some help getting out of here. After that, we crawl and pray that they haven't found our horses."

They watched the colors fade and the shadows of night steal across the sky and the surrounding mountain peaks. When Pete saw the first star appear, he knew that it was time to go. Maria helped him to stand and then she pulled him out. She disappeared for a moment and when she returned, she explained. "I wanted a gun, too."

Pete nodded. The dead mustanger sure didn't need it anymore. "All right," he said, standing on one leg and throwing an arm across Maria's shoulders. "Let's get out of here."

They each held a gun in one hand and yet managed to progress quickly across the open space until they reached the rocks that shielded their horses from view.

"We did it," Maria whispered. "I knew we could."

Pete was just about to agree when he saw something move in the shadows. He knocked Maria aside and fired as he went down. Twin blasts of muzzle fire answered and Pete rolled, firing twice more. Maria's gun barked, too. The desert echoed their gunfire across the hills and, for a moment, all was still.

Pete climbed warily up on one leg and hopped forward until he was standing over two dead men. They were lying sprawled across the rocks, and though he could distinguish their features in the moonlight, they were the faces of strangers. When Maria reached his side, they heard distant shouts and then the sound of something crashing through brush in their direction.

"Let's get out of here fast," Pete said through teeth clenched with pain.

He could feel the warm flow of his blood and knew that the leg wound had been torn open again. When he tried to reach for his animal, it smelled the blood and pulled back sharply, dragging him off-balance. He hung on until Maria could grab its halter and settle it down. After that, she was able to hold the animal while Pete got his foot up into the stirrup. He managed to throw his bad leg stiffly over the cantle.

Maria was astride her horse a moment later and they were riding blindly through the night as more gunfire erupted behind them. It was all Pete could do to hang on and keep from falling. He had no strength left in his body and when they had gone a mile or two, he called out, "Stop!"

Maria pulled her horse in and grabbed the bit of Pete's own animal. "We must go on! They will soon realize we have gone and follow."

"I know. But use my rope to tie me in the saddle in case I pass out. Then take my reins and lead it at a gallop. Don't look back until we reach the doctor in Yerington!"

Maria did as he asked. She tied his boots to the stirrups and his hands to the saddle horn. They could hear angry voices that carried in the night.

"Your leg is bleeding again. We need to stop and rest."

"We'll either rest behind a locked door tonight, or not at all," he said. "As soon as we get to town and I'm with the doctor, you'll need to find the sheriff. Tell him what happened. We must have his help."

"I will," she promised. Maria tore more bandages from her skirts and rebandaged the wound even tighter. Then without another word, she remounted and took the reins from Pete's horse and wound them around her saddle horn.

She set off at a gallop that sent wave after wave of agony radiating through Pete's weakened body. And sometime during the next few miles, he slumped forward and gave himself over to the forces of pain and darkness.

He awoke in a hotel room and the sun was shining through the windows. Maria sat beside his bed, slumped in a chair, her eyes closed, her breathing slow and regulated to the condition of sleep.

Pete's leg was heavily bandaged with cotton and tape. That said a doctor had worked on him sometime during the night, but he remembered nothing. Pete closed his eyes for a moment. Where were they? Yerington. Yes, probably in its only two-storied hotel. Today, he would have to answer questions about the death of Jenkins. And what would he say? That they were ambushed, sure. The problem was, he could not point an accusing finger at either Tyson or Lester Barron and shout, "They are the men who killed Jenkins and tried to kill Maria and me."

I have no proof. His mind was greatly disturbed by this conclusion yet unable to fathom any way to satisfy justice for himself and Maria.

A loud knock on the door snapped Maria's head erect and she stumbled for the door.

"Wait a minute," Pete said. "Give me a gun first."

Maria shook herself into full wakefulness and realized that she had almost opened the door for whoever stood outside. She gave Pete a gun and moved to the door. "Who is it?"

"Sheriff Don Jackman. Open up!"

"Go ahead," Pete whispered. "But stand back from the door when it swings open."

The door flew open and the sheriff found himself staring

into the barrel of a Colt .45. Pete studied the man's tin badge and then lowered his own gun to the bed.

"You're damned jumpy," the sheriff snapped. He was well dressed and in his early fifties. He looked altogether much too prosperous for a small-town lawman.

"We have reason to be. Hugh Tyson and his men ambushed us yesterday out in the Wassuk Mountains. There's a dead man and a stallion to prove we were mustanging when it happened."

"Yeah. That's what your wife told me last night about two in the morning. It could have waited."

Pete blinked. "No, it couldn't! What are you going to do about it, Sheriff?"

The man had a long waxed mustache he kept stroking. It was clear he resented anyone challenging his authority or judgment. "I sent a deputy out to bring the body in and search for evidence."

"And what about Tyson and Lester Barron?"

"Unless my deputy has some proof, then it's your word against theirs. And seeing as how Mr. Tyson is paying taxes and contributes to some of the local charities while you contribute squat, I think your charges are worthless."

"But they tried to kill us!" Maria raged. "Your deputy will see what happened."

"Oh." The man smiled. "I'm sure he will. And I don't doubt for a minute that you were ambushed. Not the first time it's happened. That chestnut stallion you and this Jenkins fella got your ropes on? That horse was being hunted by a lot of men. I figure one of them saw you, got mad and tried to get even."

"They shot the chestnut!" Pete raged.

The sheriff was unflappable. "So? I seen a lot of men so ornery they'd rather have an animal—or a woman—dead before it belonged to another man."

He leaned on the doorjamb. Dropping into an almost confidential tone, he said, "Pete, you and Maria are up against the biggest cattle rancher in these parts. I know that Mr. Tyson has a quick temper when he drinks, but if I were you, I'd not go making wild charges that you can't prove against the man. The smartest thing you could do right now would be to just move on as soon as that leg heals."

"Get the hell out of our room," Pete growled. "You must be on the dole."

The sheriff flushed with anger. Hands on hips, he shouted, "God damn it, I won't stand for that kind of talk. Not from a worthless saddle tramp like you."

Pete lifted his gun. He didn't need to point it at the man, but the implication was clear enough for anyone to read.

Sheriff Jackman got out fast.

The more that Pete thought about it, the more he decided that the ambush had been Lester's idea. Ambushing just wasn't Tyson's style. He was not the kind of man to wait out in the rocks all night so that he could potshot you in the morning. No, Tyson was big, blustery and as honest in his own game as a fresh deck of cards. He'd kill you if he thought you needed killing, but he'd do it face-to-face and take his own chances. Jack Kendall said that his ex-mustanging friend had turned bad, but never lost his nerve. And there was one more reason why Tyson wouldn't have been hidden out all night at that mountain waterhole—the man never strayed far from a fresh and plentiful supply of whiskey. That had been rugged country and a long ride from Cross T headquarters, a ride he doubted that Hugh Tyson would have undertaken drunk or sober.

Now Pete knew that Lester would come tonight to kill them. He wouldn't be alone and he wouldn't knock before entering. I've got to get out of here, he thought, before they arrive.

Late that afternoon, he sent Maria down to the lobby with a ten-dollar bill and a tearful story for the desk clerk. She was to tell him that they had quarreled and she wanted her own room across the hall. When Maria returned, she had the key to their new room clenched in her fist and a rather sheepish look on her face. In case Lester was suspicious enough to ask, the hotel clerk had bought their quarrel story hook, line and sinker.

They waited until after dark and changed rooms when the hallway was empty and everyone had gone to dinner.

Pete held his wife in the dark, airless room. For the first time, he sensed she was really afraid. If he thought she might have gone on the afternoon stage to Carson City without him, he would have asked her.

"You might have to kill them," she said.

"That's a possibility, but I think it more likely they'll barge into our other room and then I can jump across the hall and lock them inside. If they try to come out, I'll riddle the door while you go for the sheriff."

"It sounds reasonable." Maria gave a little shrug of her shoulders. "So why don't I think it will work?"

"I don't know," he said. "But running away isn't the answer. This is the best that I can think of."

Their room slipped into darkness and trapped the heat of the day. With the windows closed, there was no movement of air and the room was stifling. Down in the street they could hear laughter and the faint tinkle of a piano keyboard. A horse whinnied. There was a quick dogfight in the back alley that ended when someone cursed. One of the dogs howled in mortal pain.

Pete could feel sweat trickle down his backbone. He knew that his plan was crude and simplistic. A hundred things could go wrong and he wasn't at all sure he could trust his bad leg to propel him across the hallway quick enough to slam the door on Lester and his friends.

Those things were critical and a great cause of worry but, of all the fears he carried through those long evening hours, the greatest by far was that Maria might get hurt or killed. To imagine her being shot was to feel his stomach double up like a fist and slam him up under the heart. Maria had stuck it out with him so far and God knew that it had not been easy. They had mustanged from sunrise to sunset. Spent twelve to fifteen hours a day on horseback until she had tears running down her cheeks out of her weariness and saddle sores. There had been nights when he had needed to lift her out of the saddle, and mornings when he'd lifted her back into it again. Maria deserved better. Other than those few days they had spent in Reno during the fair and horse race, their nights had been on hard ground under cold stars.

She had never complained. Not once. She had risked her life for him and only yesterday had saved him from Lester's fire. Now they were alone here in this hot, choking room waiting for a bunch of gunmen. Maria was scared and had every right to be.

Pete squeezed her tightly. "As soon as this is over," he said, "we'll go to Elko and find Jack. This fall, we'll fix up our new place so it will be nice."

"Jack said he'd put in a floor for me," she whispered. Then, laughing softly, "And a roof, too!"

"You deserve 'em both. If it hasn't got a rock fireplace, we'll build a good one before winter sets in. I'll even hammer together a new outhouse if the old one has a bunch of black widow spiders."

"Thank you. That is important to a woman."

"Important to a man as well," he said earnestly, recalling more than one unwary cowboy who had gotten bit in the privates by a black widow and been out of commission for weeks. "Maria, it'll be nice for us there. You heard what Jack said about all the mustangs we can catch together."

"I heard. Would you do one other thing for me?"

"Name it."

"I want you to plant a line of cottonwood trees around the cabin for me. Just like at the Cross T."

"You bet I will. First thing."

"No," she giggled, "first the roof, then the new outhouse and then the floor. Trees are number four on my list."

"You're number one on mine." He started to kiss her and that was when he heard the protesting stairway.

Maria heard it too and froze in his arms. Pete disengaged himself. "You stay back out of the line of fire," he whispered. "Promise me?"

"Yes."

He suddenly felt a whole lot better. He wished she would agree to climb under the bed and hide, but that would be asking way too much.

Pete dropped silently to the floor and pulled himself across the room to the door. It was unlocked and he waited until he heard the men halt outside. There were urgent whispers but he couldn't make out what they were saying. The gun in his hand felt slippery and he knew he was perspiring as much from fear as the heat. He pulled himself erect to hang by the doorjamb and listen to his heart banging in his chest.

The door across from him splintered under a tremendous blow but apparently did not break open because they had to strike it again. When Pete heard it slam against the interior wall, he pushed his own door open and staggered into the hallway. There was enough light to see a trio of men standing in his former room. He saw a knife lift in silhouette against the curtains and then arc downward into the bundle he'd created by stuffing his coat and saddle blankets underneath the covers.

"Freeze!" he shouted as he lifted his gun.

Pete shot the two nearest as they spun to fire their weapons. At less than five feet away from him, he could not miss. The man with the knife whirled from the bed. It was Lester Barron and he lunged with his knife. Pete tried to swing his gun around between them but his shot went a little wide and only creased Barron's ribs. The man was still plenty alive and would have skewered Pete, except that a bullet ruined his aim.

Pete felt himself going over backward with Lester on top of him. In the dim kerosene light of the hallway, he saw that knife flash, ready to slice down into his chest. Pete threw a forearm up and blocked the thrust. Their arms locked. Once before they had fought and Pete had been victorious, but that was when he was at full strength. Now, after losing so much blood, he was weak and the knife was edging toward his throat. He tried to get his other arm up but it and his gun were pinned under Lester's knee. Pete thrashed but the knife kept inching downward.

A gunshot seemed to explode right in their faces. Pete tasted gunpowder. Lester screamed. His body lifted. A second bullet struck him and he careened over backward in the hallway.

Pete heard a sob and the sound of a gun hit the floor at almost the same instant that Maria dropped to his side.

She was crying and somehow he found enough strength to wrap his arms around her and whisper, "You did it again, darlin'—you damn well saved my bacon."

CHAPTER THIRTEEN

Sheriff Don Jackman was in a foul mood and he made no attempt to hide the fact. It was the second night in a row that he had been called out because of Pete Sills; when he found three dead men on the second floor of the hotel, he was livid.

"I may have to arrest you on suspicion of murder," he snapped. "God damn it, I wish you and your wife would have gone to some other town instead of mine!"

"He was bleeding to death," Maria said pointedly.

The lawman wasn't listening. "Why didn't you go to Carson City?"

"Because I couldn't have made it," Pete said, trying to control his own temper. "You know who these men work for, don't you?"

"Hell yes, and it doesn't make me very damned happy, either!"

"You don't get paid to be happy," Pete snapped. "As you can see, they came to kill us. All three are shot from the front—not the back. They busted in our room and Lester tried to stab me to death."

"But you outsmarted them, isn't that right? You laid a trap and when they stepped into it, you shot them down."

"I told them to freeze and they decided to shoot me instead. It was self-defense."

"That isn't what Mr. Tyson is going to want me to say."

Maria's lips tightened. "Who is the law in Yerington, you or Tyson?"

Jackman opened his mouth, then clamped it shut. "I want a full account of this in writing. Mr. Tyson is going to want to see that justice is done and, if I have to find you, you'd both better be here. Run, and I'll figure you are guilty as sin."

"I can't run," Pete said. "By the way, what did your deputy find out yesterday when he went to get Jenkins's body?"

"I don't know yet. He hadn't gotten back when I went to bed. I'll question him tomorrow morning. Hell, I'll question you tomorrow morning! Right now, I'm going to bed."

"What about them?" Pete asked, pointing to Lester and the other two dead men across the hallway. "You just going to leave them?"

Jackman knuckled his sleep-starved eyes. "Yeah," he snarled. "The undertaker and the judge are one and the same and he don't like to get up in the middle of the night either."

Pete shook his head in disbelief. "Close the door on your way out, Jackman."

"Do you think he might really try to arrest you for murder?" Maria asked.

"He would if he could. But three against two is long odds and no one is going to believe that Lester and his friends didn't come gunning for us."

"I can hardly wait to leave for Elko."

Pete nodded. "It's sounding better every minute.

They slept late and it was midmorning before they awoke. Maria went down to the dining room to eat and bring him up breakfast. When she returned, she had a plate of ham and eggs and Pete discovered he was famished. "How much money do we have saved up?" he asked, finishing his coffee.

"About three hundred dollars."

It was even more than Pete had hoped. "Maybe, as soon as we're cleared to leave, we ought to buy us a buckboard and a harness horse. We could tie our own saddle horses on the back and strike out for Elko right away."

Maria's eyes lit up with excitement. "That's a wonderful idea!"

"Then it's decided. As soon as the doc says I can travel without pulling open my leg wound, and everything is cleared with the sheriff, we'll head out. You'll have to run around and shop for the buckboard, horse and harness. And enough supplies for the trip."

"I'll start this morning."

She was so excited that Pete didn't have the heart to tell her that he would probably need at least a couple more days to mend his wounded leg. As it was, he had no doubt that the buckboard ride would be a torment.

"Try and buy one with good springs."

"I'll shop for a buggy," she told him firmly. "A buckboard ride would kill you."

He knew she was right, but he'd never thought he'd own one of the things. They were for rich and old people—not a mustanger. But he guessed they could sell or trade it in Elko for something more practical.

At noon, he was alone in the room when he heard a loud banging on the door. "Who is it?"

"Hugh Tyson. Let me in, god damn it!"

Pete reached over to the bedpost and drew his gun. He did not think Tyson would come in shooting, but the man was completely unpredictable when drinking. "Hold on a minute."

He had trouble getting across the room to the door and

when he reached it, he said, "I'm going to unlock it but don't come inside until I tell you. Cross me and I'll blow a hole in you the size of the doorknob."

Tyson cursed but the sound of his boots told Pete that he had backed to the far wall.

Pete hobbled over to a chair. "Open it and come inside with your hands up."

Tyson slammed the door open and stood framed in the doorway. Pete was shocked at his haggard appearance. The man had aged ten years in ten months. Heavy drinking had broken the veins in his nose and cheeks so that they were bright red. His face was drawn, big pouches of skin hung beneath his eyes and his cheeks were sunken. He was no longer heavy with fat and muscle, but, instead, thin and haunted-looking. With his skeletal hands resting on his hips, his ruined face was as hard as granite and just as unforgiving. "You killed them," he rumbled. "Shot them down right here in this hallway."

"They came to kill Maria and me. You've sunk to killing mustangs; are you also ready to kill women?"

"I kill my own snakes," the man rasped. "And I always have."

"You've overstocked the range and a hell of a lot of your cattle will die before it rains again. A few mustangs aren't going to make any difference."

"They do to me." His lips curled down at the corners. "You could have been somebody, Pete. I gave you a chance and you spat in my face. Now look at you!"

"And look at yourself. A year ago you had friends and the finest mustanging outfit in Nevada. But you became greedy and threw it all away. You ran off your only real friend and . . ."

"Jack Kendall stabbed me in the back! He was in love with my wife!"

The man was trembling with fury and his words were hurled at Pete like spears. "I know that," Pete said wearily. "Hell, everybody on the Cross T knew Jack loved her. But he never did anything about it and that makes him a friend. A man of honor."

"Never did anything?" Tyson's laugh was a cruel joke. "Did I hear you right? Because if I did, you don't know but half of the story. She was in love with him! Too decent to admit it, but she was and it killed her."

"I don't believe that," Pete said in a still voice. "Candy once told me her mother hated the West and died of loneliness."

"Candy was wrong. Her mother died of a broken heart and that set me to drinking and hating Jack Kendall. I blame Jack for killing her!"

He relaxed and smiled in a way that made the hair stand up on Pete's back. "And that's why I made sure that he's coming back."

Pete stiffened. "What do you mean?"

"I had a couple of men at the fair. It was pretty easy to find out that Jack is working in the Ruby Mountains around Elko."

"So what?" he asked, almost holding his breath.

"So, I sent him a telegram a couple of weeks ago saying you needed help real bad. I'm betting he'll show up any day now on that palomino. And when he does, I'll hang the bastard for horse thievery and then beat that palomino to death."

"Jesus Christ!" Pete whispered.

"He won't help either one of them," Tyson said confidently. "I'm going to let you and Maria ride out of this country. I'll give you two days. After that . . ."

Hugh Tyson left the door open and walked away. Pete heard his footsteps on the stairway. He jumped out of bed and struggled into the hall, then reached the top of the stairs. "Where did you tell him to meet me!"

Tyson looked up at him with that terrible smile and started laughing.

Maria found a buggy and they left the hotel that same afternoon, despite the sheriff's warning that he'd consider it an admission of guilt. It was an unusually cool day, with high, gauzy clouds wind-torn across the sky. Pete knew that he would never forgive himself if he and Maria let Jack ride into Tyson's trap. No one could say exactly how long it might take for Jack to receive that telegram. It could be weeks, or the same day the message arrived in Elko. The only thing that Pete knew with certainty was that, once the man read it, he would come running.

Pete and Maria had speculated about where Tyson had instructed Jack to come until their minds ran in circles. The more they theorized, the murkier everything became. Obviously, Jack would have to cross the Walker River somewhere north of Walker Lake if he were heading directly for the Cross T. Pete did not even want to think about the fact that Tyson might have arranged the showdown near Reno, Carson City or someplace in between.

When they reached the Walker River, they made camp and waited. Pete's leg was throbbing with pain but the wound had not reopened. He asked Maria to chop him a forked branch and he spent the entire first day fashioning himself a crutch. There was a high summit not far from their camp and they soon spent every waking hour up there scanning the northeastern horizon, searching for a big man on a palomino that was riding into a trap.

The days passed slowly, but Pete was determined to use them well. He had asked Maria to buy them fifty dollars' worth of cartridges and now they spent hours practicing with his rifle and their six-guns. Almost from the beginning, Maria was surprisingly good with the Winchester. She was much less comfortable with Jenkins's Colt .45. The trouble was, the Colt was too heavy for her to shoot accurately with one hand. Pete had her practice using two and that seemed to help. For his own part, he practiced drawing and firing to increase his speed. Outgunned and outnumbered, he thought that if it came to a showdown, he might be able to get the drop on Tyson and avoid a bloodbath. After firing three hundred rounds, he found that the Colt seemed lighter and that he could draw and fire from the hip without shooting recklessly. He would, however, never be a gunfighter; his hands were too rough from working mustangs and ropes and his knuckles too frequently crushed and broken. But even so, he felt that he was improving until he was considerably better than the average working cowboy. He proved this to his own satisfaction one afternoon when he had to draw and blow off the head of a rattlesnake. The act had been instinctive, totally effective.

From their summit vantage point, it seemed as if they could observe the entire sweep of the world. The earth rolled into an infinity of mountains and valleys and it all was pressed down by the monstrous expanse of blue sky. Twice, they saw Indians but Pete was not greatly concerned. The strength of the Paiutes had already been broken by the flood of whites seeking fortunes on the Comstock Lode.

Every few days, a band of mustangs returned to drink from the Walker and graze along its grassy banks. They were thin and when they galloped into the dry expanse, their dust hung for hours against the sky. Pete and Maria fashioned a sun shade of brush yet, because they were up high, even on the hottest days they were cooled by an afternoon breeze. Far to the west, he could see the hazy purple

Sierra Nevadas and they were no longer adorned with a white mantle of snow. Western Nevada was locked in the grip of a drought and it suffered.

Had it not been for the fear of missing Jack, those might have been some of the finest days of their lives. As it was, their eyes ached with the constant search for a horse and rider. Twelve days after their arrival, they did see a man on a light-colored horse, but just when they were certain that it was Jack, the rider turned west and they saw that the horse he rode was a buckskin.

Pete found he could not sleep down by the river. The sound of the running water would obscure the drum of Sun Dancer's passing hoofbeats. He moved his blankets up to the summit and the next morning Maria came to join him.

From the day he had carved his crutch, Pete had taken to notching it in order not to lose track of the time. Now, after twenty-four notches, he began to wonder if Tyson hadn't lied to him. The man was diabolical enough to invent this sort of a ruse to get Pete out of Yerington. This accomplished, it would appear that he had run to avoid a conviction for the murder of Lester and his accomplices.

We will wait one more week and then head for Elko, he thought when he awoke on the twenty-fifth day. We will either intercept Jack, or learn that Tyson never even sent a telegram and that he intended to set me up for murder.

Pete started a breakfast fire. They were almost out of supplies and down to less than fifty rounds of ammunition for the Winchester and their six-guns.

It was early. Sunrise was glowing on the eastern horizon and the day would be hot. Pete looked to the northeast as much out of habit as anything. Suddenly, he went rigid. A thin, shivering curtain hung like gold dust across the prairie. The curtain appeared in the general direction of Elko and disappeared perhaps five miles to the south along the river.

Could it be! He grabbed his crutch. In his haste, the coffeepot full of water that Maria had carried up from the river spilled across the fire and it sizzled into angry extinction. "Maria," he yelled. "Maria!"

She rolled out of her blankets and when she saw his face she rushed to his side.

"Look!" he said, pointing. "Someone passed before daylight. If it weren't for this land being so powder dry, his dust would have settled hours ago."

Her eyes tracked the curtain into obscurity. "We have to go," she said, echoing his own thoughts. "We can't stay here and take the chance it isn't Jack."

"I know. But it could be anyone. There are four or five gold rush towns to the south."

"I'll hitch up the buggy."

Pete shook his head. "No. I can sit on a horse now. I have to."

He threw his crutch into the river and managed to get into the saddle by sheer force of will. His leg throbbed but he felt no wetness and knew that the wound had not reopened.

They left their buggy, harness horse and camp as they shot out of the cottonwoods, racing downriver.

Pete did not know how far ahead the rider might be, yet it was obvious that he had been traveling fast enough to kick up a dust trail.

A betting man would have considered it long odds that the anonymous rider had been Jack Kendall. Pete was not a betting man. And something deep down in his gut told him that they had missed Jack and Sun Dancer. And maybe, God forbid, they were already too late.

CHAPTER FOURTEEN

Pete reined his winded horse in after splashing across the Walker River. "There," he said, pointing to fresh hoofprints in the mud. "That's where he came out!"

They followed the tracks up into the hills and saw again the shimmering trail of dust. Pete squinted and said, "Whoever it is, the man is heading straight for Cross T headquarters."

"But is it him!"

Pete studied the hoofmarks. "Big horse wearing no shoes and coming at a jog from the direction of Elko. I'd say the odds are that it was Jack all right, and that he passed us about two hours before daylight."

There was still another fifteen miles to go and Pete forced himself to keep a tight rein on his animal. Jack had taught him that the fastest way for a rider to travel long distances was at a steady jog. Most men galloped until their horses began to stumble, then stopped and rested them until they got their wind back before galloping again. That was wrong and a damned good way to ruin any animal; a horse ridden stop-and-start wouldn't hold up for much of a distance.

But the temptation to gallop hard was almost overpowering. The miles seemed to crawl by and it was midmorning before they were finally within a mile of the Cross T Ranch headquarters.

"Hold up," Pete ordered. "We can't just go charging over

the hill. They'd shoot us out of the saddle before we even cleared the brush and reached the ranch yard."

Pete's eyes swept across this land that he knew so well. "I think we ought to separate right now. You swing to the south, I'll come in from the north. You know that low hill behind the ranch?"

"The one with the . . . graves?"

"Yes. Tie your horse behind it and sneak in the rest of the way on foot. Here. Take my Winchester. You're as good a shot as I am with it. Give me Jenkins's six-gun."

She took the rifle but it was clear she wasn't happy with the idea of them separating. "Will you promise to wait until I can get in position behind the ranch?"

He nodded.

"Then I'll do it," she said.

Pete managed a tight smile. "This thing is going to work out all right, Maria. We haven't gone through as much as we have already to get ourselves killed just yet."

"I know. But just remember, no matter what happens, I love you."

Before he could tell her that he felt the same, she was galloping south. He admired the way she sat a horse. Straight and proud. She had worked most of her life cleaning and cooking, but you wouldn't have known that seeing her in the saddle right now. Maria was the kind of woman who learned fast and well.

Pete dismounted, keeping most of his weight on his good leg. He tightened the cinch on his horse, talking softly to calm his own ragged nerves as well as those of the animal. He checked both of his six-guns. When Maria was finally out of sight and his mount was breathing normally, he crawled back into the saddle.

Tyson had sworn to hang Jack Kendall. He was not a man to make idle promises or delay what he considered revenge long overdue. Jack might already be hanging from one of those big cottonwood trees, and if he wasn't, he soon would be.

"Maria, I'm sorry to have lied to you," he said, talking to himself, "but I can't wait and I don't want you trading bullets with anyone."

He yanked his hat down tight on his forehead and then he spurred his horse over a low hill and streaked through the sagebrush, heading straight for the Cross T.

He was still a mile away when he realized what was going on at the ranch. "My God," he whispered, "they're hanging him right now!"

At that distance, Pete couldn't have distinguished the mustanger from the six or seven men surrounding him, but that golden palomino he was astride was unmistakably Sun Dancer. The big palomino had a pair of outstretched ropes around its neck and was being held in place by two horsemen.

Pete leaned low and kept his weight up on his horse's withers. The brush was thick but they were flying. Now he could see Hugh Tyson draping the hangman's noose around Jack's neck. The mustanger's head was up and he was hatless, with his arms tied behind his back.

Pete saw a man throw the rope up and over a heavy limb and Tyson grabbed it, then handed the end to a third man on horseback who dallied the rope around his saddle horn.

Tyson ripped off his Stetson—the dance of death was to begin.

"No!" Pete shouted, clawing for his gun and firing blindly down at the group.

They whirled at the sound of his gun. For at least two heartbeats, Jack Kendall was forgotten as several of them drew their own weapons and returned fire across a distance that was still beyond the range of a six-gun.

Tyson alone understood Pete's desperate attack as a diversion. He whipped his Stetson down across Sun Dancer's haunches and the animal jumped forward. Jack was yanked over his mount's hindquarters and suddenly he was dancing on the end of the rope.

Pete screamed in helpless fury. He could see the mustanger's powerful body jerking and his legs kicking wildly.

One. Two. Three. Four horrible seconds passed, each seeming like years before Pete did the only thing he could think of that might yet save Jack's life. He threw himself out of the saddle, hit the earth and rolled. He came up and steadied his six-gun across his left forearm and aimed high at the man with the hangman's rope dallied around his saddle horn.

He squeezed the trigger and saw the man's hat fly off. The rider panicked and released the rope and Jack dropped, staggered and then leaped into the trees. Pete fired again and Tyson grabbed his arm as a bullet spun him halfway around.

"Shoot him!" Tyson screamed. "He's only one man. Get him!"

The Cross T men came weaving and dodging across the open ranch yard. Pete tried to cut them down; he uselessly emptied the rest of his gun. At the perimeter of the ranch yard was sage and the gunmen dove into it and began to advance on him. Now only Tyson and the two riders trying to keep Sun Dancer under control remained targets. But each time Pete raised to fire, a probing volley of lead began to cut the brush around him to pieces.

To remain where he was was to invite certain death. Pete knew he had to move fast in order to stay alive. He began to crawl on his hands and knees in a direction that was diagonal to the ranch house; he hoped his course would get him past Tyson's gunmen.

Gunfire from the yard brought his head up again and he saw Tyson fire twice at Jack, who came at him in a rush. Head down, legs pumping, the mustanger must have known he had no chance to escape Tyson and had elected to die fighting.

Pete could almost feel Tyson's bullets ripping into his own body and he shouted helplessly. Still wearing the hangman's noose, Jack's head slammed into Tyson and he drove the rancher backpedaling into Sun Dancer. Tyson's arms were windmilling and he grabbed the palomino's mane and tried to keep from falling.

Sun Dancer reared in terror and knocked the rancher to the earth. Tyson screamed. The scream abruptly ended on a high pitch as the mustang's hooves stomped out his life.

Jack crumpled to his knees and then pitched forward. Pete got up and began to run. He was dimly aware of the sound of a Winchester blanketing the ranch yard and scattering the unequal six-guns. The two mounted riders who had been holding Sun Dancer threw off their dallies and took off like a couple of bats out of hell.

Pete reached Jack and tore away the constricting hangman's noose. He dragged the mustanger around behind a tree out of danger only moments before Maria reached his side.

They were safe for the moment but the mustanger was dying. Tyson had drilled him twice through the chest and Jack's tortured breathing produced an ominous whistling sound from his ruptured lungs. Pete cut the bindings from his best friend's wrists and leaned close.

Jack's hand struggled up and fastened itself behind Pete's neck and his frothy-red lips moved for a moment before the hand fell away and Jack died.

Pete choked. He felt an overpowering urge for revenge as he straightened and tore the Winchester from Maria's hands. He stood, savagely levered another shell into the chamber and stepped out from behind the cottonwood tree. He had a rifle; the men in the brush had pistols. He would kill every damn one of them before sundown.

They knew they had lost. One of them tore off his undershirt and found a stick to raise a white flag. Pete raised his rifle and took aim on the man's heart.

"No!" Maria cried, grabbing the Winchester and pulling it down as the man dropped back into cover and yelled, "We want a truce! Tyson is dead and so is the mustanger. It's finished. Let us go!"

Pete allowed Maria to take the rifle and heard her shout, "Go then! All of you!"

"But we need . . ."

Whatever he needed was forgotten as Maria sent a bullet screaming over their heads.

Pete moved slowly toward the trembling palomino. He talked to it like Jack would have, despite a suffocating inner violence so strong it almost gagged his throat. Sun Dancer's eyes rolled but when Pete collected the rope and gently eased nearer to the animal, it seemed to remember again from the earliest days of its gentling that here was the other man who could be trusted.

He touched the horse's muzzle, worked his hand up behind Sun Dancer's ears and began to scratch them slowly. Tears were streaming down his cheeks when he touched Jack Kendall's saddle and said, "It's going to be all right now."

They galloped out of Cross T and did not stop running until Pete reined Sun Dancer in on the crest of a distant hill. The ranch house, its expensive belongings and the crushed body of Hugh Tyson were engulfed in flames that now reached fifty feet into the cobalt-blue sky. A pillar of thick gray smoke rose so high it could be seen for miles.

But Pete scarcely paid any attention to the burning house because his eyes were riveted to the hillside and the fresh unmarked grave that lay beside that of Candy's mother. Sheriff Jackman would come and find that grave. He would naturally assume it belonged to Hugh Tyson and it would rest undisturbed.

Jack would have his dying wish; to finally lie beside the woman he had never stopped loving.

"What are you thinking right now?" Maria asked, studying his face.

"I was thinking of something Jack Kendall once told me." Pete took a deep breath and tasted a hint of autumn on the wind. "He said that if a man died having had one good woman, one good friend and one good horse, he should feel privileged to have lived so well."

A smile formed on Pete's lips as he turned to look at Maria. "Jack had all three."

"And so have you," she told him in her gentle but proud way.

He nodded, knowing it was true. Then he reined Sun Dancer toward Elko. He had a roof to mend, a floor to lay and a new outhouse without black widow spiders to build for Maria. Oh yes, and a lifetime of mustanging together.

ABOUT THE AUTHOR

Gary McCarthy is the author of the Darby Buckingham novels published in the Double D Western line, as well as several other Western novels. His most recent work is *The Last Buffalo Hunt.* He lives in Ojai, California, with his wife Virginia and their four children.